WRECKING BALL

LINDSEY POWELL

Lindsey Powell

Books by Lindsey Powell

The Perfect Series

Perfect Stranger

Perfect Memories

Perfect Disaster

Perfect Beginnings

The Complete Perfect Series

Part of Me Series

Part of Me

Part of You

Part of Us

Control Duet

Losing Control

Taking Control

Games We Play Series

Checkmate

Poker Face

Dark Roulette

A Valentine Christmas

Games We Play: The Complete Series

Stand-alone

Take Me

Fixation

Don't Look Back

Wrecking Ball

Chapter One

Kat

EVERY GIRL DREAMS ABOUT IT.

Every woman plans it.

The white dress.

The pretty flowers.

The handsome man waiting at the altar.

And that is the most important part.

The guy. The one you want to spend the rest of your life with. The one that will cherish you, love you, protect you and make you feel like they would move heaven and earth to make you happy.

Yeah. That guy.

Except, I'm not marrying that guy.

Instead, I'm stood next to the devil with a fake smile plastered on my face.

I'm wearing the dress and I have the pretty flowers, but that's as far as it goes. The rest has all been fabricated.

You see, I'm stood here because of a debt. A debt I stupidly thought I could repay with money, but no. Instead, I'm paying with my life, and it's all my fault.

I lost and gambled away my own future.

Crazy, huh?

That it may be, but it's happened and here I am.

I'm not marrying the man I love; I'm marrying the most dangerous guy in the country.

Nate Knowles.

Number one asshole and blackmail extraordinaire.

I had a debt with the most powerful man in the crime world, and I truly believed that I could have paid him back… until I didn't.

One wrong choice was my downfall.

And that choice I made was for love. A love that turned out to be false. The man I thought I loved turned his back on me and left me to rot.

And now, here I am.

Bowing down to the crime lord where his world involves popping a bullet in someone's head as if it is as normal as eating breakfast.

Playing ball is what will keep me alive.

Acting the part is what will stop me from being fifty feet under.

So, even as I hate Nate Knowles with a passion, I will smile and say the right things in public, but in private, all bets are off.

I need a plan, a way to get the hell out of this nightmare.

I need to suss things out, ingrain myself so deep that he will never see it coming.

Role of a lifetime.

Good meets evil.

And I will take down the monster.

You just see if I don't…

Chapter Two

SIX MONTHS EARLIER

Kat

I WAS MINDING my own business, sitting in my office, looking at the books and wondering how the hell I'm going to keep my bar afloat when all it is doing is haemorrhaging money that I don't have… I was minding my own, trying to deal with all the shit in my head… No money, fuck all customers, no Clark because he's upped and fucked off—leaving me to deal with everything—no phone call, no note, no goddamn words from him… and then Nate fucking Knowles walked in to make my day even shittier. Not only do I have the brewery breathing down my fucking neck for their pound of flesh, but I've also got the most dangerous man to walk the earth sitting in front of me with a smirk on his face because he knows that I can't give him shit.

He knows this business is on its knees.

He knows that I can't pay up, and I guess my time of reckoning has come.

Except… it hasn't come in the form that I thought it would. I figured I'd be led away, maybe cop a bullet in my head for a quick release from all of the stress I have carried around with me for the last few months. But no. Instead, Nate the Crime Lord has strolled in here like he owns the place and thrown down the gauntlet…

"So, you want to make me a deal?" I ask, flabbergasted that I may just survive another day.

"Yes," he replies, his dark tones doing nothing to ease the worry in my mind.

"But I didn't pay up in time," I say, wondering what alternate universe I have woken up in to be given another lifeline.

"I am fully aware of that fact, Miss Wiltshire." Oh damn. The way he says my name makes me shiver with… nerves? Excitement? Probably both with an added sense of fear chucked in for good measure.

"And why would you do that?" I ask, dreading what the answer may be whilst still being intrigued.

He chuckles as he sits in the seat opposite me, on the other side of my desk, and fucking hell, the noise alone is enough to pull you in and make you want this man for your own… if he weren't an asshole who is only out for himself, of course.

"Because I want to fuck you," he says, his eyes dark, his lips pulled together in a straight line, the chuckle he let out seconds ago long gone.

My mouth opens and closes like a fish out of water. Seconds tick by and turn into minutes as silence engulfs us.

He wants to fuck me?

What the hell?

In another lifetime, I'd probably have been quite happy to jump on his dick… I mean, he's gorgeous, there's no doubt about it. Those sea-green eyes are captivating, that chiselled jaw just begs for me to run my tongue along it, those broad shoulders are made for my fingernails to dig in as I ride him, that black hair is begging to be tugged and have my fingers entwined through it as we come hard together… and then that ass is something straight out of a catalogue where only the buffest men grace the pages. And the tattoo I can see, snaking its way up the side of his neck and stopping just below his ear… Christ, I need to get a grip.

"I can see that you are struggling over there, so let me break it down for you," he starts as he sits there, dominating the room. "I want to own you, command you and break you. I want you to need me like you have never needed anyone before. I want to be your everything and more," he says, his sea-green eyes fixated on my light-blue ones.

"Why?" I whisper as I try to calm my racing heart.

"Why not?" he counters, looking as cool as a fucking cucumber.

"*Why not?*" I repeat back to him, my voice not hiding the emotions running through me. "*You've just said you want to own me, command me and fucking break me… Forgive me for being more than a little confused about what the fuck is going on here.*"

"*First of all, we're going to need to get that potty mouth of yours under control. I'm not going to have my wife dropping f-bombs all over the place,*" he says, and I feel like the wind has been completely knocked out of my sails.

"*Wife?*" I question. "*You want me to marry you?*"

"*Yes.*" No further explanation, just a simple '*Yes*,' as if that settles things.

"*No way. Not happening,*" I say, shaking my head from side to side, my eyes wide with shock.

"*Well then, Miss Wiltshire, it seems that you have two options. One, you become my wife and live a fairly decent life where you will have protection and security, or two, you die. The choice is yours.*"

Choice?

I don't have a fucking choice! Is he crazy? Of course he is. He's Nate Knowles, crime lord and total nut job. I was an idiot to get into bed with him in the first place, so to speak.

"*Be my wife or die, the choices are laid bare, nothing hidden,*" he says, and I can't help the sarcastic laugh that leaves me.

"*Nothing hidden?*" I muse. "*You don't expect me to believe that bullshit, do you?*"

"*Again with the vulgar words,*" he says as he stands, buttons up his suit jacket and walks around to my side of the desk until he is stood beside where I sit. He turns my chair to face him, leans down and places his hands on either side of my chair, closing me in, encasing me as his delicious scent invades my senses. And as he leans down, his lips become level with mine, and I can't help but notice how full they are. My heart races, my blood pumps, and my pussy tingles, because clearly, she wants what is right in front of me, even as my head fights against everything this man represents. Death, violence, crime… it's so far from my world… and I need to stop looking at his body because I could easily let myself loose on this man. I bet he fucks hard and… For God's sake, stop it, Kat.

I quickly move my gaze back up, but when I connect my eyes with his, I fear it was a mistake. His eyes are hungry, I can see it. He sees me as a fucking toy that he can destroy, but he doesn't really know me and I'm not going to let some *crime lord believe that he is going to kill my spirit. I'm determined, just like him, and if I have to become his wife in order to survive, then so be it.*

If I gain his trust, I can ruin him, just like he's trying to do to me.

"You have twenty-four hours to make your choice," he says in a deep, low voice before pushing away from me and making his way to my office door.

"Wait," I call out as his hand pauses on the door handle. He slowly turns as I make my way over to him, until I am standing in front of him, looking up, admiring how bloody handsome he is. If only he wasn't an asshole that likes to fuck with people's lives.

I think of my bar and how I've worked my ass off for years for it all to come to nothing.

I think about how Clark has totally screwed me over and how he just ran away because he's a goddamn coward.

I think of my shitty apartment where I've been scrabbling to meet the rental payment every month because Clark never helped me do shit.

I think about how stupid I was to stay with Clark and how it's led me to this moment.

Marry a crime lord or die.

Dear God, you couldn't make this shit up.

And as I realise that I am going to have to kiss goodbye to my current life and adopt a new one, I open my mouth and speak before I have a chance to change my mind.

"I don't need twenty-four hours," I say, determination coursing through me. "I'm in."

Chapter Three

Nate

KAT WILTSHIRE. A woman that any man would be lucky to have. A woman that I am marrying in mere moments. Except, I'm not lucky, I'm not her soulmate, but she is mine, and I will do everything I can to fucking break her and make her see that I am the only person she will ever need. Seems drastic, but she's fucking stubborn, and I look forward to smashing those damn walls she's built around her. Walls that should never have been put up in the first place, but then, we all make shitty decisions at times and I guess her ex was one of hers. Fucking Clark. I mean, even the name is a shitty one, let alone the decision to spend your life with a total and utter fucking leech of nature.

She doesn't know the half of what that douche bag did, and I have no plans to tell her, unless she pushes me of course, which I expect in my attempts to break her.

Yeah, I sound like a dick, and I'm okay with that. Because in order to save her, I have to break her first, but she isn't going to know that.

In fact, she is going to think I'm her worst fucking nightmare.

As I wait for my bride-to-be to walk down the aisle, I cast my mind back to the moment I first laid eyes on her...

"BOSS, YOU HAVE A VISITOR," Stefan—my right-hand man—says as he comes into my office with a suspicious smirk on his face.

I throw down the pen I was writing with and sit back in my seat. "And who is it?"

"Oh, I'm not making any introductions for this one," he says before he disappears, and I refrain from calling him back because he's just walked off and is about to let fuck knows who in here without giving me any details on who the hell it is.

I'll be having fucking words with him later. This is not how we do shit. I like to know who thinks they can walk into my territory and think they have a free pass to come into my office—which on this occasion, I guess they do, because of Stefan. Fuck's sake.

But all thoughts are halted as an actual goddess appears from behind the door, looking like Bambi caught in headlights for a few seconds before her eyes connect with mine and she schools her features.

Jesus.

Long brunette hair that is left down and framing her face, a slight tan to her skin that almost glows, curves in all the right places that instantly make my dick want to go exploring, full lips that just beg to have your tongue run over them and your teeth nibble them as you work her into a frenzy... and those eyes... light blue's that have an array of emotions swirling in them. Determination, feistiness, doubt, nerves, excitement... And those tight jeans, come-fuck-me ankle boots and sleeveless shirt that has a couple of buttons open at the top but in a classy way rather than a slutty way... Jesus, fuck.

She seems to snap out of whatever daze she was in and fixes me with a hard stare, her emotions shutting off, and in its place, nothing but confidence. She walks further into the room, her jaw clenched, her chin lifting slightly as she comes to a stop in front of my desk, and I allow my lips to pull into the smirk that I had been holding back as I looked up and down her beautiful body and naturally gorgeous face.

"Mr Knowles, my name is Kat Wiltshire, and I am here to ask a favour of you."

Her voice is like fucking music to my ears.
This woman is sex on legs and then some.
And her words bring me nothing but joy.
"I am here to ask a favour of you."
This is going to be fun…

THE MUSIC STARTS TO PLAY, and the guests begin to stand. There are a fair few here because I am a fucking crime lord, so if people get invited to my wedding, they come, no questions asked.

I turn around as the doors open fully and watch as my bride stands there, the light framing her like an angel. I have to control my jaw from dropping because she is fucking stunning. Wearing a gorgeous cream dress that highlights her perfect curves and shows off her slightly tanned shoulders, I have to admit that I did fucking good when she failed to pay up. Her long brunette hair is curled around her face, hanging loose, just begging to be wrapped around my hands and pulled as I fuck her senseless.

And then there is her face. Her beautiful face which she has kept as natural as possible, but let's be truthful here, the woman doesn't need any make-up. She's naturally gorgeous, and she doesn't even realise it, which just makes her even sexier.

Yeah, I hit the fucking jackpot, and it's a damn shame that I have to break her in order to make her see that it is only me who can own her heart, her body, her mind, and her soul.

She begins to walk down the aisle to the music, each footstep bringing her closer to me. God, I could literally pick her up like a damn caveman and carry her out of here, but I won't because I have a job to do and a show to put on. So, I school my features, keep my face straight, all the while keeping my eyes on her.

Kat Wiltshire.

My wrecking ball.

She's going to try and fight me; I can see it in her eyes.

That's okay though, because it makes it more of a challenge, and a challenge is always sweeter when won.

You see, I'm going to be an absolute bastard to her, I'm going to make her hate me, make her wish that she had died rather than chosen to be my wife.

Why?

Because I'm a sick fuck that needs to break those that get this close to me in order to make sure they are all fucking in. I can't have room for doubt. I won't allow myself to be burned by anybody, not even her.

She's getting closer, and I am so ready for this to be over and to start our new life together.

Her light blues sparkle despite the fact that she hates me. I know how good I look in a suit, and it shows on her face. We're going to have to work on her poker face, make sure she keeps those slight twitches hidden from predators. She's going to need to hone her skills, and I'm going to help her.

She stops in front of me, and I take a moment to just appreciate her.

Even her fucking cheekbones are perfect. Such a shame we couldn't have met before now. Before my heart became stone and my tolerance for bullshit was at an all-time low.

I study her lips—her full, plump lips that are slightly parted and begging for me to devour her. I reach my hand up and brush my fingertips over her cheek. I don't miss the blush that creeps up her neck and her eyes closing for a brief second as she allows herself a stolen moment to savour my touch.

I lower my voice and whisper so only she can hear. "You ready to do this?" It's the one and only time that I will show her a softer side of me.

She holds my gaze and I see the indecision in her eyes. I know this isn't the way she would have chosen to get married. I took that choice from her, and I don't care. She's mine, and today will seal the deal.

"Yes," she whispers as she blinks away tears that threaten to fall.

"Good," I say before dropping my hand. "Let's get on with it."

Kat

"Let's get on with it."

I scoff as I replay those words over and over in my head. Fucking poetic, I think not. Fucking romantic, not in any way, shape or form. I am so over today. My wedding day. The first official day of hell.

I should be with a man that I love, but that asshole fucked me over and left me to the wolves. Nate Knowles being the wolf—and now my husband. The asshole being Clark.

I bring the glass of champagne to my lips and knock it back, placing the empty glass down on the table and picking up another one.

"Take it steady, my love," Nate says, his lips by my ear, his hand covering mine that rests on the table, curled into a fist. "Wouldn't want you to ruin your appetite by getting pissed."

I drain the glass and place it down on the table before turning to look at Nate. "Wouldn't want me embarrassing you, more like," I counter, my tone not hiding how irritated I am.

"I expected the bite to come a little later than this, Kat, but I have to say, an hour after our wedding is impressive."

"Don't act so surprised, Nate. You're not stupid and you know that I didn't want this," I grit out through clenched teeth.

"You had a choice."

"Yeah, a totally shit one where I could either marry you or die," I seethe, keeping my voice low, because as much as I hate him, I would hate for people to pity me more.

"Forgotten that potty mouth of yours?" Nate remarks.

"Not at all. I'm an adult, a thirty-two-year-old woman who can say what she damn well likes."

"Not anymore," he says and grips me with his steely gaze. "My wife will be respected, not looked at like a piece of filth because she can't keep her mouth in check."

"You want me to keep my mouth in check?" I say as I move closer to him, my lips brushing over his as I speak. "Never going to happen, husband. Maybe you should have thought about that before you forced me to marry you." I get up before he can reply and push my chair back before walking away from the table and out of the ridiculously extravagant mansion that we are having this fake-as-fuck meal in.

I march down the steps and across the grounds, kicking my heels off as I step foot onto the gardens that wrap around the whole place. I need some air and I need a moment. I stop when I am out of sight, hiding my body behind a bush and closing my eyes for a second to stop the frustrated tears from escaping.

You know those guys that you want to choke but fuck at the same time? Yeah, that's how I feel about Nate, because as much as I hate him, I want him, and I despise myself for it.

My head is a clusterfuck of emotions, and it's about to get a whole lot more clouded as I feel hands being placed on the tops of my arms from behind me. I know it's him before he even speaks.

"What's wrong, wife?" he whispers, his lips right by my ear, his breath whispering over my skin. I fight the delicious shiver that wants to race through me because I can't let myself be completely his. He trapped me into whatever this life is that I am about to begin, and for that, I will always hate him.

"Just needed some air," I manage to choke out.

"You know, this doesn't have to be hard, Kat," he says, and I break away from him, putting a few steps between us and turning around to face him, hands on my hips. He puts his hands in the pockets of his trousers, and fuck me, I have never seen such a dominant, glorious sight in all my life. Damn my pussy for tingling at his mere presence.

"Don't come out here and try to sweet talk me, Nate. You made this happen, and I had no choice but to come along for the ride. The question I can't seem to answer though is why... Why on earth would you want to do this to me?" I rush out and instantly regret saying anything as he stalks towards me, his eyes igniting with a fire that I don't want to respond to, but my damn body seems to love.

He stops just in front of me, eradicating the distance that I put between us mere seconds ago.

"I already told you. I want to own you——"

"Yeah, yeah, own me, control me, and make me need you. I get it. You want to screw with my brain for failing to pay a fucking debt—" My words are cut off as his hand comes to my throat, his fingers wrapping around as he gently squeezes.

"I told you to watch your mouth," he warns, but all that does is send heat racing to my excited pussy.

I can feel tears clogging my throat, but it's not because I'm scared, far from it. It's because I know that I could easily fall for this guy, even though I know all he wants to do is break me down and make me weak.

"Despite what you might think, Kat," he begins, loosening his hold on my throat a little, letting his fingers massage my skin. "I haven't done this to make your life hell."

"No?" I scoff before I can stop myself.

"No." His eyes blaze, and for some reason, I know he's telling me the truth. Now I just have to figure out why he chose to spare my life and make me live his. "In time, you will learn to get along with me, but for now, all you have to do is keep your mouth in check and live the high life."

"Ah yes, because you're Nate Knowles, crime lord and all-round badass alpha," I say, sarcasm lacing my tone.

"Yes, I am, and it would do you good to remember that," he says before letting go of me completely and turning and walking away.

I watch his retreating form and admire his broad shoulders before focussing on his ass.

Christ, I need to get a grip.

I am going to be totally screwed if I allow my womanly wants to take over everything I stand for.

I will be nobody's toy.

I'm not here to be owned by some guy that thinks he can have everything he wants without consequences.

I am my own person and I intend to stay that way, and I need to make sure I blind-side the bastard, so he doesn't see my exit from his life coming.

Chapter Four

SIX MONTHS EARLIER

Nate

"I KNOW what I'm doing, Stefan," I tell my right-hand man—soon to be dead man if he keeps bloody questioning me about what I'm doing with Kat.

"You sure, Nate? Because I know you, and I know that there is another reason for doing this," Stefan continues, pushing me a little bit more.

"I told you, I have it all under control," I bite out.

"But—"

"Will you just fucking stop!" I shout as I stand up and bang my fists on my desk in anger. *"I do not need to be questioned, I know my own goddamn mind and it has decided that I want her as my wife. End of fucking discussion."* It's that simple. I want her and I got her.

My eyes narrow on Stefan, the closest person to me, as I try to rein myself in.

Stefan holds his hands up, palms facing me in surrender. *"Okay, I get it, you're fine. You're so fucking fine that you just slammed your fists into the desk and gave me the bloody death stare. Me. Your closest friend. Your best friend. But hey, who am I to question the great crime lord, Nate Knowles, in making one of the most bizarre decisions ever,"* he says before letting his hands drop to his sides.

"Stefan—"

"No need to tell me to do one, Nate, I'm already out of here." And with that, he opens my office door and leaves, closing the door quietly behind him.

I let out a sigh and sit back in my chair, my mind feeling like it's going to explode with all the questions going round and round like a fucking Ferris wheel at one-hundred miles an hour.

Stefan and I have been friends for years, and there isn't much that gets me pissed off at him, but when it comes to her, I will piss on any prick that stands in my way.

Kat Wiltshire. The woman of my goddamn dreams, and the one I have to break in order for her to truly see the bigger picture where we could be happy, a couple, a team. She took money from me six months ago, was meant to pay it back and that be the end of it, but she couldn't pay me, and I know it isn't really her fault. Doesn't mean that I am willing to let her go. Not now. Not ever.

I know the money was for her and her ex-douche-bag bloke's shitty bar that was making zero profit. I also knew that the business was totally fucked and unsavable when I leant her the money. Her ex is one slithery snake, but when he put her in my path, I had to become somewhat snake-like myself. You see, I've admired Kat ever since she walked into my office, and I've never wanted to fuck anyone more.

I'm a man that gets what he wants, and I want her.

Only thing I need to do is make sure that I don't break myself in the process, because fuck if she isn't the only person who could ever do it.

The amount of power she has, and she doesn't even realise it.

The way in which I have shunned other women because I knew that I didn't want a life of quick pussy and torrid affairs.

She ruined me the moment I set eyes on her, made me see just what true beauty was. I'm not one of those men that chase skirt constantly, looking to sink my dick into the nearest hole.

I've never really been a fuck boy, and no, I'm not some soppy twat that has been pining away for her for the last six months. I just knew that I never wanted to settle. But for her, I am.

Nate Knowles is going to be wed. She accepted my offer last night. Not that she had much of a choice, even I know that, but she said yes and now I'm planning everything. The only thing she has to do is go and get a dress.

We're going to be wed in six months.

She has one week to wrap up her existence and kiss goodbye to that shitty bar and everything she knows.

Life for her is about to change dramatically. I won't bother her for the week, but when it's time to collect, I'll be there, waiting.

She's going to hate me.

She's going to want out.

But sometimes, we hate those that we love.

Sometimes, we don't accept the inevitable until it is thrust into our face.

I say I want to break her, and I truly mean that, because in order for her to accept me, she has to see the darkest parts of me. I've done some truly terrible shit, and I harbour ghosts that will never leave me. I've tainted, I've maimed, and I've tortured.

To truly accept someone, you have to see them as a whole, and she's about to get one hell of a life lesson.

Kat

One week.

One week to say goodbye to my life and enter his.

I'm so fucking screwed, and I have no idea how to get out of this.

I've wracked my brains for an out. I've thought about begging, getting down on my knees and asking him for mercy, but I know that won't do any good.

He's a bad man, and we don't share the same principles.

I could kill Clark—my ex—for doing this to me. He's the reason my life is in tatters. I have no idea what happened or where things went wrong, but it did, and it has. He left me high and dry to pick up the pieces, and I'm paying with my life. I'm not sure if death would actually have been a better option.

I'd been with Clark for four years. I thought we were happy. I thought we were building a future, but all he was building was a fucking gambling habit and making me his cash cow. It was his idea to go to Nate. He persuaded me, he pushed the fucking trigger on my life, and he's not even here to see the consequences. He disappeared two weeks ago. I realise now that that wasn't a coincidence. He knew our deadline to pay up was coming to an end, so he took himself off in order to save his ass. Bastard. Four fucking years I gave to him and he deserted me.

Now I'm left with the devil, wondering what the hell his reasons for doing this are.

Chapter Five

Kat

I WALK BACK into the extravagant room and take my seat next to my husband. Dear God, it's like something out of a fucking nightmare.

Here I am, in a room full of some of the nastiest men and women in history, and I'm married to the fucking crime lord that runs it all.

Couldn't make this shit up if you tried.

I've been living in his world for months now, no job, no purpose, just there to escort him to whatever function he needed me to. I'm a nobody, a nothing, and the realisation hits me with a pang. I feel the tears welling in my eyes and I furiously blink, trying to keep them at bay. I lower my head, because as shit as this all is, there is a part of me that doesn't want to embarrass myself or Nate by being some teary-eyed wreck.

But as soon as my chin touches my chest, I feel his hand take mine—the one resting on my thigh. His fingers gently entwine with mine and I close my eyes for a second, taking a couple of deep breaths.

I don't know what it is he does to me. Like I said, I hate him, but then there are these moments where he surprises me. Like now.

His other hand comes to my chin and lifts my head up, turning me to face him. For a second, I think that he's angry, pissed off that I'm sat here looking as miserable as sin at my own wedding, but it's not anger that I see, it's something else I can't quite put my finger on. And then he surprises me in a way I never thought possible as he moves closer, and his lips connect softly with mine.

I'm momentarily stunned by the action.

We've never kissed before, not like this. Sure, he's placed a kiss on my cheek, and we had a brief connect of lips at the altar after saying our vows, but this is different. This is more, and I have no idea what to do with that. My body seems to answer for me as my eyes close and my lips decide to enjoy whatever this is.

The way he moves his lips against mine—so soft and gentle—is making me want to put aside all of my previous thoughts about him. I'm too vulnerable right now to push him away. It's a very stark realisation that he is the closest person to me. He's one of the only people I've seen in months. He's the person I talk to daily, no matter how much I try to avoid it. He's the one I eat dinner with every evening, the one I hold hands with when required, and he's also the one that sleeps in the room across from me every night…

FUCKING HELL. His house is huge. Massive. Ridiculously oversized, but I can't help but be astounded by the sheer size and beauty of this place.

I've never set foot in somewhere so plush. The interior designer must have had a field day when they did this place, because I can't imagine for one minute that Nate chose the décor or the thick carpet that your feet sink into. He just doesn't seem the type—given that he is too busy offing people in his daily life.

Even the woodwork of the banister has intricate detail as it leads upstairs to more large rooms. Nate is giving me the grand tour, and when we come to a stop outside of two doors—one on the left and one on the right—I hope to God that one of them is a bedroom for me because there is no way that I am sharing a bed with him, wife or not.

He opens the door to the left and gestures for me to walk in. When I enter, I see a king-size bed with gorgeous bedding adorning it, and then two more doors—one opposite the bed and another to my left.

"That door leads to your walk-in closet and the other to your ensuite bathroom," Nate says as he points to each in turn.

"This is my room?" I question, because I don't fully believe that he is going to give me this amount of space, even though I've been hoping for it.

"Yes."

"So, this is my safe space?"

"Kat, this whole fucking house is your safe space," he tells me, and my eyes lock with his.

"Safe space or prison?" I question, one eyebrow raised.

He chuckles and the sound does nothing to dampen the fact that despite what he is making me do, I still wouldn't mind fucking him.

"You know, you're getting a pretty good deal here. I could make you sleep in my bed; I could make you conform to all my wishes, but with time, I know you'll get there on your own," he says, and I scoff.

"Oh please, you're living in a dream world," I retort, because as much as I may want to fuck him, I'll never do it.

"Never hurts to dream and then work like fuck to get what you want," he says, his easy demeanour changing in an instant.

"Hmm. I guess when you have the means to threaten others to get what you want, it's easier, huh?" I say, because I can't help but bite back at him.

I don't fail to miss the clench of his jaw at my words.

He takes a step closer to me, and another, until he's leaning down slightly so that we're eye level. "If it helps people to see what they truly can become, then yes."

I suck in a sharp breath.

Is he talking about me?

Before I can respond, he straightens himself back up and says, "My room is the one across the hall," before he waltzes out and disappears down the hallway.

I turn in a circle, my eyes roaming over every bit of the room again.

So, this is my life.

Plush surroundings and a husband-to-be that confuses me at every turn.

Great.

. . .

HE NEVER MADE me sleep in the same bed as him, giving me my own room to help me feel like I had a safe space. That was the first glimpse at a softer side that I saw from him.

There haven't been many tender moments between us, but this one right now will forever mark my memories.

And when he pulls his lips away and brings the hand that was holding my chin to my cheek, cupping it and brushing the tear that has escaped away with his thumb, it makes my heart ache because this isn't real. This is some sick game that I am a mere participant in, and that makes me want to cry a goddamn river.

I bite my bottom lip hard to stop myself from showing him anymore weakness.

"Half an hour and then we can leave," he says quietly, his eyes not leaving mine.

I nod my head and then the moment is over as his hand drops and we both turn towards our guests.

Our guests.

Our life together, and it's all a lie.

Nate

Fuck. Seeing her upset makes me wonder what the hell is going on in that head of hers. She looks so fucking miserable, and I know that it's because of me, but I also know that I won't let her go. So, for my sins, I will suffer seeing her like this until I make her cry with laughter.

One day, this will all make sense to her, but not yet.

I haven't even begun to show her the real world we all live in. She needs to see it and realise that there are very few people you can count on in this life. Most are out for themselves and will put their life above yours. People are selfish, and I guess I'm no different. But I'm only selfish with her because I need to be.

Twelve minutes until I can get her out of here.

Twelve minutes until we can go home and she can try to shut herself off from me again.

That kiss just now was unexpected. I didn't have a plan to kiss her like that, and I sure as hell didn't expect her to respond. But now I know that she doesn't completely hate me, and I have to work on that in order to get her to see that I am not the monster that she thinks I am.

Eleven minutes and counting.

The plates have been cleared away and the guests are drinking their final glass of champagne before they switch to spirits for the remainder of the evening. I won't be here to see it, and I couldn't give a shit, if I'm being honest. Highly unpractical to leave your own wedding early and miss the evening part, but my life is anything but practical. I do what I want, when I want, and no fucker will ever question me about it. Except maybe Stefan, but he soon gets told.

Stefan is sat the other side of me, and I turn to him and inform him that we will be leaving in nine minutes time. He gets up and starts to prepare our men for our exit.

This may be a wedding, but there is no way I was taking any chances—today of all days—when it comes to safety. There are men out there that want to gut me like a fish, so my guys are always on hand to watch my back, and now my wife's.

Eight minutes. I am starting to wonder why the hell I didn't just fly us out of here and to some private beach where we could have gotten married on the sand, the sound of the waves in the back-ground, and no fucking people there to bother us.

Seven minutes, and oh fuck me, here comes Zoey. Jesus, she's like a bloody noose around my neck at times.

"Hey, bro," Zoey says as she slides into Stefan's seat by the side of me.

"Zoey," I say, knowing damn well she's seen Stefan doing the rounds and that she is going to try and keep us here.

"Don't be so bloody formal, Nate, it's me, your sister, not the fucking queen," she says, and I hear a soft chuckle from the other side of me. I'll take that over Kat's tears any day. Zoey is thirty-one and full of fucking mischief, and I don't need her bringing that mischief around my new bride. Zoey can be very persuasive when she needs to be, and I don't think it would take much for her and Kat to form some sort of fucking alliance just to try and get under my skin.

"Why are you preparing to leave already? I haven't even had a chance to speak to your wife… you know, the one you never thought to mention until the invitation came through the post, and the one I am yet to meet properly," Zoey says, her tone taking on a sarcastic edge and showing just how pissed off with me she is.

"I had my reasons," I respond.

"Which were what?"

"Never you mind." It's all she's getting because in four minutes, I'll be out of here and away from her interrogation.

"Not good enough, Nate. We're family, and family should stick together," she says.

"Yes, Zoey, they should, but it's not always the case, as you full well know," I bite back.

"Don't you dare bring up fucking Lucas at your own wedding," she scolds me, and I instantly know that I have fucked up by even hinting at a man that should have been here today. Lucas. Our brother, and the bastard that killed our mum and dad, hoping that he would take control of their empire. Little did he know that the empire was always meant for me.

Lucas hurt both of us when he killed our parents, and then he tried to twist the knife in further by framing me for a drug deal gone wrong. Luckily, I had an alibi and Lucas didn't cover his tracks very well, so his shit plans went up in smoke. Shame he isn't burning in hell along with his shitty plans. He escaped and has clearly gotten better at planning because I can't track the shady fucker down, but I will, one day. I will never give up looking for him because he deserves to pay for his sins, and I want to be the one that collects.

Two minutes.

"Have you been listening to a word I've been saying?" Zoey says, breaking me from my thoughts.

I stare at her blankly and she rolls her eyes at me.

"For goodness sake's, brother." She sighs. "I'll be round tomorrow night at eight."

"What for?" I ask.

"For dinner, duh."

"You can't."

"Why the hell not?" she says, and my eyes flit to the clock to see that I have one minute before I can be out of here.

"Sorry, sis, gotta go," I say and stand up, grabbing Kat's hand and pulling her up from her seat. She looks shocked as I position her next to me, my arm around her waist, pulling her in close to my body. Dear God, she fits next to me like a glove.

"Nate," Zoey says as she pouts and crosses her arms over her chest.

"Talk soon, sis," I say with a smirk as I whisk my bride away and across the room to where Stefan is waiting by the door.

Kat doesn't say a word as I take her outside and into the car waiting.

I shake hands with Stefan—who escorted us out—and then we're off, down the driveway and heading in the direction of our home to start our new life together as man and wife.

Chapter Six

Kat

I DON'T KNOW what I'm feeling... well, I do, but I know that I shouldn't be feeling anything for the bastard sat next to me. My husband. My fucking keeper—because that is what he is, and that is why he has me here. To keep me. To make me suffer, all in the name of a goddamn debt.

But just now, before we got into this car, he was different.

That kiss.

The genuine look in his eyes.

The way he made me feel something other than disgust... ugh, as I said, bastard.

I keep my eyes trained out of the window, not wanting to risk looking at him because I'm scared of what I might see.

I saw it back at the wedding reception... the slight hint of something other than hate.

I've never actually asked him if he hates me, I've just presumed that he does because there is no other reason for wanting to make me marry him against my will.

If we had met on different terms, then maybe things would have been different. I mean, there is no denying that he is handsome, sexy, and charm personified—and he bloody well knows it. His sea-green eyes, his perfectly chiselled jaw with slight stubble, his broad shoulders, his muscular physique and his perfect ass… I'm not blind and I can appreciate a handsome man, but what I can't appreciate is this whole scenario.

If we had met in a bar, at a restaurant, in a goddamn club, then maybe things could have been different, but they're not and here we are, both about to embark on a fake-ass marriage that will probably end up with us both being utterly miserable.

Great.

Adulting at its finest.

I watch as the scenery passes, people walking hand-in-hand, groups of youngsters hanging out, a few people on their own just walking and passing the time to get to where they need to go. And here I am, in a wedding dress, and I should be feeling like the happiest woman in the world, but I'm not.

I've never been someone who bows down and takes shit from anyone… well, anyone except Clark because he shit on me from a great height and left me to face the music. I already feel like I am going to become someone that I hate, and I don't know what to do with that.

I wish I could speak to Clark and ask him why… why the hell did he do this to us? Why on earth would he betray me in such a cruel way and leave me to face the big bad wolf alone? But of course, there is no sight of him anywhere, and I exhausted all options to try and find him because he doesn't want to be found.

He couldn't help me now anyway, so there would be no point.

I guess I just feel like I have no closure. One minute he was there, and the next, he was gone.

One minute he was my life, and the next, he wasn't.

Being an only child and having no family of my own left has clearly made me more vulnerable than I realised. I thought that Clark loved me, I thought that we were happy, but clearly, he was hiding secrets that I will never know the answers to, and that pisses me off.

The rage bubbles away inside of me, mixed with sadness and a desire to be the woman that I always thought I was. I want to be strong; I want to live my life the way I choose, but plans change, and we can't all live out our life-long dreams.

Mine was to run a business with my partner, it was to settle down, have kids, maybe get a puppy and spend weekends at the beach thinking about how lucky I was… but that dream went up in smoke the day that Clark asked me to go and meet with Nate and ask him for money. I should have listened to my gut and stayed away, but with Clark's credit rating being total shit, we never could have borrowed enough money legitimately, so I had no choice but to go crawling to a crime lord.

His words have come back to haunt me every day since…

"YOU GO, it will be better coming from you," Clark said.

"Why?" I questioned.

"Because you're a hot woman and you are more business minded than me."

"Oh gee, thanks," I replied sarcastically with a roll of my eyes.

"Even if you weren't hot, you know what to say and how to talk business, whereas I am no good at anything like that," he said, sadness lacing his tone. He dropped his head, and I could only presume it was in disappointment at himself.

"Hey," I said as I moved towards him and crouched down in front of him, gently placing my hand on his knee. "Stop that, you don't need to be so hard on yourself all the time."

"I just feel like I fail you at every turn, and I'm so sorry, Kat. I wish I could be the man that you deserve——"

"You are the man I deserve," I tell him, cutting him off. "I will sort this, and I will go and see Nate. You don't need to worry about anything. As long as we have each other, that's all that matters," I tell him, knowing that I will try to ease his worries in any way that I can, and if going to see Nate helps him feel better then that's good enough for me.

"I love you, Kat," he said, his eyes glistening.

"I love you too."

. . .

PFFT. What a twat. I fell for his lies and the bullshit excuses each and every time.

He didn't love me. He used me. He made me believe that I was his whole world, when really, I was his fucking bank balance.

I hope that wherever he is, he's suffering, because that's what he deserves.

He doesn't deserve to live a good and honest life because he is a liar and an asshole. Yes, I hold bitterness because it is my fucking right to do so, and no, forgiveness isn't always the way forward. I swear to God, if I ever see him again, I won't be responsible for my actions.

"Kat," I hear Nate say at the same time as I feel his hand gently rest on my knee. I turn my head to look at him, and I hate that there is a part of me that can visualise falling for this rotten bastard.

"We're home," he says, and the word hits me like a tonne of bricks.

Home.

Man and wife.

Fuck.

I take a deep breath and the car door opens. I make my way out of the car to see that Nate's driver, Jay, is stood by the door, waiting for me to get out. I stand tall, trying to inject some life into me as Nate comes to stand at the side of me, his hand going to the small of my back.

Oh God, I can't have him anywhere near me with his intoxicating scent fucking with my senses. I move forwards and away from his touch, thanking Jay as I walk past him and to the front door of my prison for the next however the fuck long it might be until I find a way to leave.

"Thank you, Jay," I hear Nate say, and I grit my teeth as I push the front door open. We don't need to carry keys because the security knows we're here and I'm well acquainted with the security system that notifies of everyone who comes and goes from this place. I swear there is some guy sat in a little control booth just watching the fucking front door all day and night long, waiting for the moment he can push the button to open the door and have something to do. The thought almost makes me laugh as I make my way up the stairs and to my room.

I don't wait for Nate, and I have no intention of coming back out of my bedroom tonight. I don't trust myself not to give in to the fucking want that has plagued me since that kiss at the reception.

I pause a few steps away from my bedroom door and my hand moves to my face, my fingertips touching my lips as I recall the one and only genuine moment I have had with Nate. Why the fuck am I so emotional today? I've held it together pretty well over the last six months, but today, all of my bravado seems to be unravelling, and I have no idea why.

"You okay?" I hear him say from close behind me, and I close my eyes, willing the goddamn emotions to piss off so I can carry on being the cold-hearted bitch that I have become over the last few months.

I take a deep breath, letting it out slowly before replying, "I'm good."

"I don't think you are though…" he says, his voice trailing off as I whirl around, my dress swishing around my legs, my emotions ready to bubble over.

"Do you not?" I retort, hands on my hips.

"No, I don't," he says as he takes a couple of steps towards me.

"And why on earth would you think that? Because you haven't given a shit about my feelings for the last six months," I argue, getting more and more angry the closer he gets to me.

Before I know what is happening, he's on me, pushing me back against the wall, one of his hands by the side of my head, the other around my neck as he bends down slightly, his eyes coming level with mine.

"Stop with the potty mouth," he scolds, but somewhere in the last few seconds, a fire has lit inside of me, and whatever lit it needs to stay because I need to feel something other than confusion and loneliness, even if it's just for a minute.

"Or what?" I challenge him, a smirk playing on my lips.

"Don't fucking push me," he growls, his body pushing against mine, not an inch of space between us.

"But you can swear all you like?" I question.

"Yes," he replies, no hesitation.

"No fucking deal," I say with a smile on my face, knowing that this will piss him off. What I expect to get from this, I'm not sure, but I know that fire inside of me is bubbling away nicely, waiting to explode like a fucking inferno.

His face comes closer, his lips hovering above mine. If I were to push forward, we would be locking lips... why does that thought make my pussy tingle? Shit. I need to focus on the hate that I feel for this man, channel it and hold onto it forever.

"You trying to test me, wife?" he says, his voice low, dangerous, and so fucking delicious that it turns those flames up a little bit more. If he kisses me, I'm not sure that I will be able to stop it.

"I'm going to test you... Every. Fucking. Day," I reply, dragging out the last three words. I'm poking the beast, and it's the most alive I've felt in months.

"I'm warning you, Kat—"

"Warn me all you like, Nate, it won't change me, and it won't change who I am. You married a potty mouth, so fucking what? I married a monster against my will, so I guess that makes us even... you forced me into this, and I say the word fuck. Not a bad deal for you, if you ask me," I say, the bitterness now taking over everything I feel. See, emotionally unstable. One minute hot and fiery, the next bitter and twisted, and then the next, sad and lonely. Fuck my life.

He grinds his hips against me and damn if it doesn't make me want him whilst hating him.

I grab hold of his hips and try to push him away, but he doesn't budge.

"Stop fighting this, Kat," he says, his eyes boring into mine.

"Never," I say with determination. "I will never stop fighting against you."

"One day you will," he says as his hands cover mine. He grips them, and in one swift move, my hands are above my head, his holding them in place, his body crushing mine against the wall. Damn my fucking panties for becoming wet. I don't want this... or do I? Maybe fucking him will help with some of my pent-up frustration? I mean, it's been months since I've been intimate with a guy… maybe I just need some kind of release to lighten my load?

"And what makes you so sure of that?" I say as I try to quench the need to have his dick inside me.

"Because I see it inside of you. That fire. That burn. That ache for something more."

"Pfft," I scoff, but he isn't wrong. Fuck.

"And right now, I know that you're wet for me, waiting for me to take you, claim you and make you feral with desire."

"You don't know shit—"

"MOUTH," he shouts loudly, making me jump. "I know more than you think, Kat. Never underestimate me."

"Back at you, baby," I say in a sickly-sweet tone, that damn smirk back on my face. "You think I don't see the way that you look at me? You want me, but you don't get to have me, because I hate you, husband." I inject some venom into my tone, fighting every single urge to smash my lips against his.

Now it's his turn to smirk at me. "Good, because in order to love me, you need to hate me first." And with that, he lets go of me, steps away and disappears down the hallway and into his bedroom, leaving me asking for the millionth time, "What the fuck?"

Chapter Seven

Kat

ONE A.M.

I've been led here for hours, tossing and turning, replaying Nate's words over and over in my head on a fucking loop.

"Good, because in order to love me, you need to hate me first."

What the hell does that mean?

Why did he say it?

And why am I obsessing over it?

"Argh," I say out loud as I turn onto my front, burying my face in the pillow, willing my mind to just stop. But it doesn't and I'm soon out of the bed and splashing cold water on my face in my ensuite.

"Fucking man," I say to the mirror, wishing that I could vent my frustration somewhere, anywhere, anything to try and relieve the ache inside of me to know the answers to my questions.

The last six months have been so vague, despite him coming in and flipping my world upside down. I moved in, played the part when needed, but apart from that, nothing, nada, and I am so sick of getting nothing.

I dry my face, a new determination coursing through me.

He can't leave me high and dry like this.

I need answers, and I need them now.

Nate

I stand at the window of my bedroom, staring out across the grounds, just watching the stars twinkling in the sky.

That fucking woman drives me crazy.

I know that I'm probably being unfair, but I'm Nate Knowles, and no one makes me feel bad… until her.

I run my hands through my hair in frustration. The way her body felt against mine earlier was like nothing else, and that was with clothes on and her hating my very existence. Imagine if she loved me. Imagine the fucking fire that would ignite between us then.

My thoughts are interrupted by my bedroom door banging into the wall. I turn, and there she is, looking like a beautiful goddess, albeit a pissed off goddess, but a goddess all the same. Christ, her eyes are blazing, and I can just picture us going at it on the bed, on the floor, against the wall, any-fucking-where…

"What the fuck was that?" she says as she marches towards me in her itty-bitty shorts and tight tank top. Fucking hell, she's never looked so damn fine. Make-up free and all natural, she exudes the power of a red-blooded female, and I absolutely wish that she would give up the pretence of not wanting me, because together, we would be fucking dynamite.

I wait until she is stood in front of me, tits pushed forward, hands on her curvy hips, one foot tapping away as she awaits my answer.

"Watch your goddamn mouth," I scold her, and I relish in the way her eyes narrow on me. I fucking love making her mad because I'm a sucker for the blaze in her eyes when I do.

"Answer the damn question, Nate," she says, her tone all kinds of pissed off.

"I'm not sure what you're trying to ask me."

"What happened earlier in the hallway? What exactly was that?" she says, and I can see the determination coursing through her.

Fuck yeah, baby, give me everything you've got.

"That was simply a husband and wife having a discussion," I reply, my face deadpan.

"No, don't do that," she says as she points her finger in my face. "Don't stand there and make out that it was nothing."

"Well, if you're so sure that it was something more, why don't you enlighten me?"

She huffs, throwing her hands up. "Argh, you're so fucking annoying."

"MOUTH," I say to her, raising my voice.

"Why do you have such an issue with me swearing?"

"I already told you," I say in a low voice.

"Yeah, yeah, because your *wife* should be respected, blah, blah, blah."

Oh, fuck me, she really does have a way of getting under my skin. I'm going to have to find a way to keep her mouth in check… maybe putting my dick in it will help?

"It's not a good enough reason, and I call bullshit on all these goddamn rules you seem to throw out when you feel like it," she continues, and I stay quiet as she works herself into some sort of frenzy. "I am my own person. Despite what you say, you do not own me, and I can say and do whatever the hell I want.

"You don't get to be an asshole and then show me a moment of affection like you did earlier at our wedding reception, you don't get to trap me in this life without giving me an explanation—"

"Except I can, and I have," I interrupt her, and fuck if the fire doesn't blaze in her eyes a bit more.

"And it's not right. None of this right," she fumes. "I don't want to be some little wifey that keeps her mouth shut and gets down on her knees when it suits you. That's not me, Nate. I don't know how to do this…" Her voice trails off and it's like she's stuck in her own torment. I can see the frustration and confusion on her face. She doesn't know what to feel, and as her husband, maybe I should make that right? Or is it too soon? I have no fucking clue, but I know that I don't yet own her soul, and that is something I need because I am a fucking control freak, and when I love, I love hard, so giving her my heart is going to require more than what she is giving me.

"I can't be this person. I feel like I'm losing my goddamn mind and I don't know how to stop it," she carries on speaking, her eyes focussed on the wall behind me. "Six months I've been here, and not once have you shown me affection like you did today, and I don't know what to do with that." Her head drops and I feel something uncomfortable stir inside of me. Christ, what is that? Compassion? Guilt? Fuck no, it can't be...

"I don't want to feel like I'm just here for your amusement. I don't want to be treated like some good little pet that may get the odd pat on the back for behaving themselves. I can't do it, and I don't want to.

"This isn't how my wedding night was supposed to be. It was supposed to be magical, one night where my husband showed me how much he loved me, and vice versa. I wasn't meant to be sleeping in a room on my own whilst my husband was in another."

I said I wanted to break her, and I think I'm starting to witness it happening. It's sooner than I expected, but something has made her crumble tonight. I've made her crumble tonight. For her, I've taken away her dreams and replaced them with a nightmare that she will be living for the rest of her days. Because she is never leaving me, and I will make damn sure of it. The only thing is, am I ready to end her nightmare and be the man that she deserves?

My body makes the decision for me as I move towards her, taking her face in my hands and tilting her head up to look at me.

"Don't," she says as she tries to shrug out of my hold, but all that does is make me hold onto her a little bit tighter.

"Kat—"

"No," she says, and this time she rips herself away from me, moving a few steps back. "You can't do this to me, Nate."

"So you've said, but I'm not doing anything."

"You are," she says, and more tears start to fall down her face. "But you're too stubborn to see it."

It's the last thing she says to me before she turns and walks out of the bedroom door, closing it quietly behind her.

Chapter Eight

Nate

"YOU'VE BEEN HERE for a couple of weeks now; don't you think that you should drop the hostility a little bit?" I say to Kat as she sits opposite me at the dining table, picking at her food.

"I play the part when you need me to, but here, behind closed doors, I will act the way I want," she retorts, spearing a piece of asparagus onto her fork angrily.

"You should be grateful," I throw out at her, and her fork slams down onto her plate.

Our eyes meet, and I can see that she would love to throttle me right about now.

"Grateful?" she says, her voice going high-pitched. *"Fucking grateful? Are you shitting me?"*

"For fuck's sake, Kat, watch your language," I scold her, my blood boiling at her use of profanities. She rolls her eyes and huffs, crossing her arms over her chest and leaning back in the chair.

"You know, you could have picked a woman who was easier to handle," she mumbles before adding, *"Just saying."*

"Trouble is, no one else owed me a debt." I smirk, loving how she makes me

feel alive inside. I've been dead inside for a long time, fuelled by my work and running a tight ship... It's good to feel emotion over something—or someone—else.

"That damn debt," she says quietly, but I hear her loud and clear.

"Look," I begin, placing my knife and fork down and giving her my full attention. "This doesn't have to be hard, Kat. We could have a great life together, but you need to stop shutting me out and start thinking of me as exactly what I am."

"An asshole?" she questions with a grin, and fuck if it doesn't make me want to burst into laughter and carry her to the bedroom like a caveman to shag her senseless.

"Your husband-to-be," I say, smug as fuck.

She scoffs and takes a sip of her drink. She has a glass of red wine whilst I have a cold, crisp lager.

"So, husband-to-be, how exactly do you want this to play out?" she asks, her eyes looking at me over the rim of her glass as she takes another sip.

"Well, for starters, we could get to know one another a little better, that's usually how things progress."

"Okay," she says, putting her wine glass down and sitting forward, her arms resting on the table in front of her as she holds my stare. "Hi, I'm Kat, my dick of an ex-boyfriend left me to face the music for a debt he needed me to take because he was a selfish jerk. I have no family left because they either died or upped and left. I like dogs, my favourite colour is red, and I hate people telling me what to do," she finishes, and then sits silent, waiting for me to make my next move.

"Good to know," I say with a nod of my head before divulging a few things to her. "My name is Nate, I'm a successful businessman, feared by most, and I love the power of who I am. I've worked my ass off to be the person I am today, and I won't ever let anyone take my empire away from me. I have a sister, parents are both dead, and I hate cats. My favourite colour is black, much like my soul, and I too hate being told what to do."

"Huh. Well, I guess that's going to make things interesting then, isn't it?" she says, and I see a hint of a smile playing on her lips.

"It sure is."

.   .   .

THAT MEAL WAS five months ago, but it seems longer somehow, the memory of it abruptly entering my head whilst drinking my morning coffee. Her fire, her spunk, it's one of the things that attracted me to her. I saw it that very first day, even as she asked me for money. I've always been a pretty good judge of character, and I got her spark spot on.

I didn't sleep much last night, tossing and turning, replaying her being in my room over and over again. It could have been so different. It could have been everything she wanted on her wedding night and more, but it wasn't, and here I am now, waiting to see how fiery my wife is going to be this morning.

I don't have to wait long as she waltzes into the kitchen and goes straight to the coffee machine, ignoring me completely as I sit at the table and watch her.

She is fucking perfection in tight skinny jeans and a sheer white blouse, with white heels to match. Her hair is hanging in loose waves down her back, and I think about how good it would feel to have her hair wrapped around my fist as I fucked her from behind.

She tinkers with the machine, setting it up and placing a mug underneath the ridiculously expensive contraption that I just had to have because caffeine is one of my vices, and there isn't anything worse than a shitty cup of coffee.

"Good morning, wife," I say to her back as the machine pours her coffee before she clicks it off and takes the mug, turning to look at me and leaning back on the worktop. She's got make-up on, but she doesn't need it. She's gorgeous with or without it.

"Morning," she says in an icy tone, her eyes focussed on mine.

"Did you sleep well?" I ask her.

"Oh yeah, like a goddamn rock," she replies sarcastically with a roll of her eyes. "You?"

"Not bad." I'm not giving her anything more because she doesn't need to know that I spent the night thinking about her and me against the wall, in the shower, in my bed…

"So, husband, what's the plan today? I mean, newlyweds and all, shouldn't we be swooning over one another and strolling hand-in-hand wherever we go?" Oh, that sarcasm is fierce this morning, and I absolutely love it.

"Is that what you want to do?" I ask her as I finish my coffee and take the mug over to the sink, placing it in the bowl before turning towards her.

"What?"

I slowly take steps to where she is still leant against the worktop. "Spend the day hand-in-hand, swooning over each other," I say as I come to a stop in front of her, my hands going either side of her, caging her in. I lean in close, my face a whisker from hers. The tension between us is unreal, and I wish to God that she would just give in and let me take her, right here, right now.

She scoffs but it holds no ground with me. I see that she wants me, it's right there, in her eyes. She can't hide it from me.

"A nice meal, a few glasses of wine and then a stroll through the park, stopping every few seconds because we can't keep our hands off of one another. And when our lips meet, it will be like nothing else exists," I whisper, the tension ramping up a few notches, her breathing a little deeper.

"You're fucking with me, right?" she whispers back as she tries to give me a death stare and fails.

"Not if that's what you want to do."

"No thanks," she replies before she dips down and under my arm, escaping me. "I'd rather gouge my eyes out," she throws over her shoulder before she disappears into the hallway, taking her coffee with her.

Huh. So I guess the emotional moment from last night has passed.

This is going to be fun.

Kat

"Dick, dick, dick, dick, dick," I repeat as I make my way back to my bedroom, thoroughly pissed off with the way that Nate speaks to me. Who does he think he is? Fucking smug bastard.

He thinks that he can get in my knickers, and that is never happening, even if my traitorous body thinks different. I can feel my pussy tingling whenever he gets close, but fuck if she's getting any from him.

I take a big mouthful of my coffee before placing it on the bedside table and sitting on my bed, throwing myself back dramatically as I stare at the ceiling.

I'm pissed, angry, mad.

I'm mad at myself for wanting him.

I'm angry at him for things being the way they are between us. The hot and cold, the push and pull, the arrogance of him needing to get his own way all the damn time.

And I'm pissed that he saw me at my most vulnerable last night.

I need to get out of here and clear my head, but I have nowhere to go and no one to call. What a pathetic life. I mean, look at me, thirty-two years old, no friends, no family, just a husband that fucking infuriates me, a husband who I despise and want to fuck at the same time, and nothing in this life to fill me with hope.

How did it come to this?

I feel my eyes burn with unshed tears and I angrily blink them away. Crying will solve nothing, so why bother?

A knock on my door interrupts my miserable thoughts.

Great. The beast has come back to try and piss me off further.

He doesn't wait for an invite as the door opens. I don't move, I stay led on the bed, staring at the ceiling. He doesn't deserve my attention.

I listen to his footsteps pad lightly across the carpet, and then I feel the bed dip bedside me.

Mother of f—

"You gonna hide out in here all day?" he asks as I feel him lay down next to me, his body an inch or two from mine.

Oh great, another moment where he can mind-fuck me and then flip the switch from light to dark once again. I'm going to have to be stronger than this to keep living this life.

"You ever heard of waiting to be invited in?" I say, ignoring his question, keeping my eyes trained on the ceiling.

"I shouldn't have to be invited in. It's my house and you're my wife," he says, and don't his words just fuck me off. I sit up and turn to face him, my face showing every single emotion because I can't hide it.

"Yes, I am your wife when it suits, when it is convenient for you, hence why you have me here, but don't think that means that you can come into my own personal space and do what the hell you want," I huff. "Who the fuck do you think you are?"

It takes him one second to move into a sitting position. It takes him another second to be on top of me, and about half a second for him to have me on my back, his body hovering above mine, his hands holding mine above my head.

"How many times do I have to tell you to watch your damn language?"

"And how many times do I have to ask you why?" I retort.

"Fucking hell, you're infuriating," he says with a sigh.

"Back at you, baby. Now just answer the fucking question," I say, drawing out the word he hates the most.

I see his jaw tense, I feel his heat rolling against me, and I wish to God that we could be different because this is like some fatal attraction shit, but in this case, I'm the only one that will get burned.

"I want to be the only person to make you scream uncontrollably, in bed, whilst I'm eating your pussy, so yeah, I want to be the only one to make you shout profanities because I am the only person that can do that to you," he says, and fuck... my knickers may just be a little bit wet.

"I will be the only person to make you say fuck with my name following after."

"Oh," is all I can say. I have no words. I have no comeback, and damn my body for getting all flustered whilst I lay underneath him, trapped by him, and wanting to be taken by him.

"You know, Kat, one day you won't hate me," he says quietly as he runs his nose down the side of my face. "One day you'll learn to love my dark heart."

And then he's up and off me and gone as quickly as he came in.

My heart is thudding in my chest from the last few moments. Jesus, can this shit get any more complicated?

Chapter Nine

FOUR MONTHS EARLIER

Nate

"NOW, remember to smile, we don't want people thinking you don't want to be here," I say to her, wishing she could fix her face to look less fucking miserable.

"But I don't," she grits out, and it gets my back up.

"You've been here two months now, so you should be getting used to things," I say, the irritation evident in my tone.

"Right, because keeping me like a caged fucking animal is the way to go," she says sarcastically with a roll of her fucking beautiful eyes. One day, I'm going to make those eyes roll in the back of her head... when I'm eating her pussy.

"Don't be so dramatic, and watch your language," I scold her. It's all I ever seem to do because she just can't keep her goddamn mouth in check. "You're hardly a caged animal either. You have the freedom to do what you please—"

"Except leave you," she interrupts.

"Yes, Kat, except leave me, so why don't you just accept it and move the fuck on?" I grit out.

She pins me with her eyes as I stand beside her. "Never."

I smirk because she has no idea how badly she is going to be begging for *me… eventually. I always get what I want, and I still want her, more now than before. Her fucking sass has my dick hard several times a day.*

I hold my arm out to her for her to link hers through. She eyes me for a moment before rolling her eyes and conceding defeat. We need to look the part, and I can feel her body tense as she comes into contact with me. I'm guessing that's a good thing. She's struggling with what her body wants and what her mind is telling her to do. I can see it, I can feel it, and I'm going to crush those fucking doubts.

"You know that one day, you're going to look back and realise how stupid it is to fight against me," I say quietly as I lead her into the mansion before us. We're here for an event for one of the charities I support, one close to my heart, and one that will probably shock Kat because despite what she believes, I'm not a total monster.

"Pfft. You're so sure of yourself," she comments, her eyes fixed straight ahead of us.

"Of course, because if you can't back yourself then what's the fucking point?"

She turns her head to look at me, tilting it to the side slightly as if in deep thought. "Huh. I never thought of it like that."

"Well, now's the time to start. Always back yourself and never let anyone tell you that you can't," I say, my eyes connecting with hers, a heat passing through me—and her if her deep breaths are anything to go by.

"Except for you, again," she says, meaning that she can't tell me no about her debt to me.

"Exactly," I say with a wink, and I see a hint of a smile on her lips that she is trying to hide.

She loves the challenge, and I am more than up for the battle.

Kat

We walk into the grand mansion in front of us, which is every bit as luxurious as you can imagine a mansion is. Large grounds, long sweeping driveway, land-scaped gardens, butlers waiting at the doors… and as we approach the inside, I can see the décor is exquisite. Mainly gold everywhere with hardwood floors and

*large chandeliers—I feel like I have walked into something out of a fairy-tale,
except I'm not with the prince, I'm with the big bad wolf.*

*I have no idea what tonight is all about because I didn't ask. I want no part
of his life, I'm merely here to settle a score and hoping he will let me out early—
unless I can find a way of escape myself, but after racking my brain for the last
two months, nothing has come to me.*

*"Good evening, Mr Knowles," one of the butlers greet as he welcomes us
inside.*

*"Evening," Nate replies, and I can already sense in his tone that he is
turning on the charm for the evening that is about to unfold.*

"May I take your jackets?" the butler says, but Nate waves him off.

"Not necessary."

*"Very well, sir. Enjoy your evening," he says with a bow and then Nate is
walking us through the expansive reception area and along a large corridor.*

*As we turn right, I see that we are in a ridiculously large room, tables lining
the outsides filled with food and drinks, people milling about in the middle, and
light chatter carrying in the air around us.*

*A few eyes come our way as we walk further into the room, and so do the
appreciative glances from women, until their eyes fall on me. Their expressions
quickly turn into scowls and I refrain from rolling my eyes. If only they knew
that I was a hostage here tonight, then maybe they wouldn't look so pissed off
that they aren't in my position.*

*I can appreciate that Nate is handsome—gorgeous even—but that doesn't
make up for his annoying as fuck personality and stubbornness. He thinks that
one day I will come to like that about him, I say he's hoping for a fucking
miracle.*

*"Nate, my boy," some old guy says as he appears through the throngs of
people. I would say he's about sixty, with a pot belly and one of those stupid
moustaches that flick out at the end on either side. All he needs is a fucking top
hat and we have our very own detective show. I stifle the laugh that wants to rip
from my throat at the thought.*

*"Sidney," Nate greets, holding out his hand from the arm I'm not hanging
off of for him to shake. "Good to see you here."*

*"Thank you for the invite," he says as he shakes his hand and the turns his
attention to me. "And who might this beautiful woman be?" He casts his eyes
over me appreciatively and a shudder wracks my body. Ugh.*

"*This is Kat, my fiancée,*" *Nate informs him.*

"*Oh.*" *Sidney clearly can't hide the look of surprise on his face.* "*Pleasure to meet you,*" *he says, now holding his hand out to me. I don't want to take his hand, but I feel like I must, so I do, and he brings my hand to his lips and places a kiss on the back of it. I stop myself from pulling my hand away even though I want to rip it from his grip. I feel Nate stiffen beside me and I wonder if he is pissed off with me? I mean, I couldn't give a shit if he is, but I don't see why he should be seeing as I'm playing the fucking part and all.*

"*Well, this is sure to be the talk of the evening,*" *he says as he finally lets me go and I return my hand to my side. I would like to go and wash the germs off of me, but that would appear rude, and for my sins, I'm so very fucking British in my manners it's ridiculous. You know, where you feel like you have to apologise even if you don't know what you're apologising for or where making a cup of fucking tea will fix everything.*

"*I don't see why it should be,*" *Nate says as he removes my arm from his and brings his hand around the back of me, his arm going around my waist, his hand settling on my hip as he pulls me flush against him. I'm caught off guard by the action and my hand comes up to land on his chest, feeling the hard muscle beneath. Fuck. No, no, no. I hate him, I hate him, I hate him. But you can want to fuck someone and hate them at the same time, right? Hate sex. Sounds fucking hot.*

"*The point of tonight is to raise money for charity and nothing more. I hope you have made a sizeable donation, Sidney,*" *Nate continues, the power exuding from him. This guy looks like he's shit his pants a little as he tells Nate that he has made a hefty donation and then he excuses himself and walks off, back into the crowds and away from us.*

Nate brings his lips to my ear and whispers, "*Never ever let yourself be alone with that man, and if you ever find that you are, be assured that if he ever touched you, I would rip his fucking dick off and make him eat it.*"

I look up at him, tilting my head slightly.

Why is my heart beating like that?

Why is there a flurry of activity in my belly?

Oh hell.

"*Okay,*" *is all I say as he gives me a half smile.*

"*Good. Now, we're here to raise money for a domestic abuse charity, one that helps to shelter women and children that need protection.*"

"Oh."

Wow. I wasn't expecting that, and I don't know what to say because I thought that we were here for his own gains and nothing more. Clearly, I was wrong.

"You ready to help me make some serious money?" he asks, a twinkle in his eye.

"For this charity? Fuck yes," I say without hesitation.

He brings me close to him, his chest against mine as he whispers in my ear, "Mouth." It sends a delicious shiver down my spine, and I have to remind my pussy that we are not letting his dick in.

He pulls back and places a kiss on my forehead before taking my hand and leading me through the people to find our first target.

Huh. Seems like I'm going to have to work harder to hate this bastard.

Chapter Ten

PRESENT DAY

Kat

I SIT across the table from Nate as we eat our dinner. It is a far cry from what we should be doing the day after our wedding, but that would require love and acceptance, and I'm not willing to give him either. I am aware that my life would be easier if I just accepted my fate and got on with it, but I'm not that type of person. I'm a fucking fighter and that will never change.

Since he came into my bedroom earlier and laid down on top of me, his heat burning through my clothes and his dick between my thighs, I have been able to think of nothing else. I need to get fucking laid, and quick if I'm ever going to stop thinking about him taking me, licking, sucking, fucking… Oh dear lord, I need to stop.

I put a piece of steak in my mouth and resist the urge to moan out loud at how delicious it is. Nate's cook sure is amazing, but I do find it odd that he doesn't just cook himself. Same as the cleaning which he employs a couple of people to do. It does my head in when they're around the house, and it doesn't help me with feeling relaxed in the slightest. Every room I seem to go in, the fucking cleaner is there. When I walk in the kitchen, the cook is there. It's not what I am used to, and I decide to bring it up because I have had a brain wave.

"Nate?" I say to get his attention as he reads something on a notepad next to him.

"Yes, Kat," he says, his eyes now focussed on mine. Christ, I could get lost in those eyes if I let myself.

"I was thinking, do we really need a cook?" I say, realising that I just said 'we' without meaning to, like we're a real couple. Fuck it.

"Why? Do you not like the food?" he asks, his brows furrowing.

"No, it's not that, it's just weird."

"What is?"

"Paying someone to come here and cook," I tell him, and he still looks baffled. I roll my eyes and continue. "Nate, I have nothing to do all day long. I'm bored, I need something to do, anything to pass the time, so I thought that I could take over the cooking and cleaning of this place."

"You want to do the cleaning and cooking?" he asks, as if it's odd that I'm suggesting this in the first place.

"Well, yeah. I have no job, no purpose, no daily ritual, so at least a bit of cooking and cleaning would make me feel like I'm doing something," I say, biting my tongue so I don't sarcastically add on that it was my life-long dream to become someone's fucking skivvy.

Nate leans back in his chair, his hands in front of him, entwined together like he's the head fucking honcho… which technically, he is, but not here. Here I need to make my mark before I totally lose myself, and if that starts with cooking and cleaning, then so be it.

"Okay," he says simply before sitting forward and continuing with his meal.

"Okay?" I say after a few seconds, wondering why he made that so easy.

"Yes, Kat. O-kay," he says, repeating the word slowly.

"Well… okay then." I look back to my food with nothing further to say on the matter. I mean, I expected to have a discussion about it, a debate almost as I expected him to say no, so I have nothing to add to the conversation.

A few seconds pass and then I hear him mutter quietly, "I knew it wouldn't take long for you to get into this wifey role."

And there it is, the asshole is coming out to play... I kind of missed him there for a minute.

"I'm just bored as fuck, Nate, nothing more," I say with a smirk because I know he's about to get all pissy about my use of the word 'fuck.'

He narrows his eyes on me, and damn if my knickers don't just become a little bit wet. This back and forth we seem to be doing is driving me crazy.

I want him.

I don't want him.

I don't mind him.

I hate him.

I love toying with him.

I hate that he plays with my emotions.

The list goes on and on and it's driving me crazy.

Maybe I should fuck him? Get it over and done with and out of my system?

"Stop fucking swearing," he says, and it isn't lost on me that he just swore himself.

I smirk and rise from my chair, walking along the table, my fingertips running over the dark wood as I get closer to him.

"Or you're gonna do what?" I challenge. He's yet to follow through with any threat of me watching my mouth, so I'd like to see what he would actually do.

"Don't test me, Kat," he says, his jaw clenched as I rock up by the side of him, perching myself on the end of the table.

"Maybe I want to," I reply, my arms crossing over my chest.

"Trust me, you don't."

"Oh, I think I do, Nate. You see, I'm just a bored and lonely housewife now, so I need to do something to make my day a little more exciting," I say as I uncross my arms and put them either side of me, gripping onto the edge of the table as I lean closer to him. He pushes his chair back slightly and I shuffle along until I am completely in front of him, my legs inches from his.

"And if saying 'fuck' in front of you spices up my day, then I'm not going to stop," I say with a wink, and then he's standing up, grabbing me from my perch on the edge of the table, wrapping my legs around his waist and slamming me against the wall to the left, his hands gripping my hips, his fingers digging in.

And then something happens to me.

Something I never expected as I whisper in his ear.

"Fuck me, Nate."

And those words are like a red rag to a bull as his mouth slams against mine, and Jesus, it's like I've died and gone to heaven as he devours me, his tongue massaging mine, his lips tasting me and mine him.

I lock my arms around his neck, moving my fingers to his hair, pulling his short locks, causing him to omit a low growl as he continues to fuck my mouth with his tongue.

Dear God, I want that tongue in my pussy.

He shows no signs of stopping the pace, and right now, in this moment, I don't want him to.

I want to just forget about all the reasons why I shouldn't do this and enjoy it. And that is exactly what I intend to do.

He moves me away from the wall, my legs still wrapped around him, my fingers still gripping his hair. His feet are moving, but I don't care where he's taking me, I just want his tongue on my pussy followed by his dick inside me. It doesn't matter that it's a guy that I hate because all that will do is bring a fierce passion like never before.

He's carrying me up the stairs, along the hallway, and a few steps later, I'm being thrown onto the bed so hard that my whole body bounces back in the air before landing and being engulfed by the mountain of a man I call my husband.

I barely take a breath before his lips are back on mine. I reach down, moving my hands to his trousers and unzipping them, keen for him to get his cock out and ride me hard. I don't know if I have ever been this turned on before in my life. He complies and moves away from me, standing at the edge of the bed as he removes his clothes one by one until he is fully naked, and fuck me, the sight before me is glorious. I mean, Adonis hasn't got shit on this man. He's got muscles in places I never knew existed. Hard ab lines, ridges everywhere, those powerful fucking arms, and then there are the tattoos that I didn't even know he had.

My jaw drops open a little, and then his voice brings me back to the here and now.

"Your turn," he says as he reaches for me, grabbing my hands and pulling me off of the bed until I am stood in front of him. "Take. Them. Off." I presume he means my clothes, and his deep gravelly voice sends shivers over my skin.

All of a sudden, I feel nervous.

What the fuck am I doing?

I hate this guy, yet I'm about to get naked for him?

I've lost my mind.

"Don't make me ask twice, Kat," he says as his eyes bore into mine.

I feel like I can't swallow, a gigantic lump forming.

And then my hands move of their own accord, undoing my shirt buttons and letting it fall down my arms before it hits the floor, pooling at my feet. Next are my jeans which I slide down my legs and step out of, so I am left in my knickers and bra.

Nate quirks an eyebrow at me. "You forgetting something?" His eyes then move down my body and land on my bra, and I gulp.

Oh, fuck it, in for a penny and all that. I make quick work of taking my bra off, throwing it over Nate's shoulder, and then I push my knickers down my legs and stand tall. I'm not ashamed of my body, and I'll be damned if I don't own it.

I watch as Nate looks over my curves before his eyes come back to mine, a low growl leaving his throat, and then he pounces, knocking me back on the bed, his body covering mine, his lips devouring me all over again as his dick nudges my opening.

He moves down my body, his mouth placing kisses in a trail as he goes, and then he's settling between my legs, looking like a guy that hasn't feasted in a long time.

"I've been waiting for this," he says before he plunges his tongue inside of me, his fingers gripping my thighs, holding them apart as wide as they will go. I don't know where to put myself as his tongue thrusts in and out of me. I don't know where to look as his tongue moves up to my clit and flicks lightly, over and over again.

Oh my…

And then he's sucking lightly, moving one of his hands and putting his fingers inside of me. I moan, I writhe, I move my hands to the back of his head as I just can't get enough. I grind against his face, needing more. He complies and sucks harder, flicks his tongue faster, and plunges his fingers in and out harder, quicker. My legs tremble as I feel myself building towards orgasm. I tug his hair, and his hands come to just under my ass as he pushes his face into my pussy harder. Dear lord, my insides feel like they are about to explode with excitement, my pussy is hungry for this, and damn if I don't feel like I am about to have the most intense orgasm ever.

"Nate—"

"Say it," he says against my pussy.

"Say what?" I pant.

He moves his lips away slightly as he replies. "I shouldn't have to tell you."

I lift my head to look at him, puzzled by what the fu… Oh…

"I'm not putting my lips back on your pussy until you say it," he says with a smirk as he sees I have understood what he means.

"Make me fucking scream, husband," I say in a low voice, and damn if those words don't turn him into an animal as he returns to feasting on me, fucking me with his fingers and working me into a goddamn frenzy.

I scream out as my orgasm surges forwards. I shout, I curse, and Nate continues to take everything from me. My whole body is trembling, the pleasure becoming too fucking much. I am about to beg him to stop because I don't think I can take anymore, but then he flips me onto my front, moving me so my knees are bent, and my ass is in his face.

I don't have time to do anything other than cry out as he slams his cock inside of me.

Oh sweet Jesus.

He rides me, his cock sliding in and out, his fingers moving around to my clit and teasing it all over again. I can't hold myself up and my legs threaten to give out, but Nate puts his arm under me, holding me in place as he continues to relentlessly fuck me into oblivion.

"Holy shit," I whisper as he speeds up, hitting me at my core.

I tense my walls around him, the only thing left I can do as my body turns to fucking goo, and then he lets out a loud roar as he reaches his peak, just as he makes me come again.

I've never had multiple orgasms during sex, let alone ones this powerful.

Our combined profanities echo off the walls before he collapses on top of me as we both pant, trying to regain control of our breathing.

And then he moves us, so I am lying on my side, his arm locked around my waist as he keeps me close to him, his body against mine as I close my eyes and forget about how I am his wife because he made me choose him or death, and instead, feeling satisfied as I let myself be taken into a peaceful sleep.

Chapter Eleven

Kat

I WAKE up feeling every part of my body ache, but in a good way. I stretch out, feeling the burn go through me, and then I realise that I am alone. Nate has gone, and I don't know why disappointment is the first emotion I feel.

Why did I think he might still be here? How stupid of me. We had a hateful fuck and then he left, the moment over.

I move from the bed and pad over to my ensuite and look at myself in the mirror. My hair is a mess, my lips slightly swollen and my face flushed. I don't know how long I've been asleep, but I can only imagine the flush has come from my mind recalling the way Nate took me. Hard, fast, deep, and nothing like I have ever experienced before.

The way in which he fucked me but made me feel like the only woman in the world was something else, and now I have to make sure it doesn't happen again.

One moment of passion was our lot, and now it's back to business as usual.

I splash my face with cold water and then brush the knots out of my hair before throwing it up into a messy bun. I leave the bath-room and go to my ridiculously large walk-in wardrobe and grab a pair of jogging bottoms, a bra and a vest top. I have no need to dress up around here. It's meant to be my home, and if I want to rock a pair of jogging bottoms, then I damn well will.

I leave the bedroom, bracing myself for whatever Nate may throw my way after last night.

The smell of the fresh coffee hits my nose first as I make my way down the stairs and into the kitchen. Nate is sat at the kitchen table, paper in front of him, coffee in hand, looking fucking edible in his suit—complete with grey shirt and black tie. If our relationship was normal, I'd be ripping it off of him and fucking him on the table, but we're not normal, so I push the thought to the back of my mind.

"Good morning," I say as I make my way over to the coffee machine.

I feel his eyes on me as I walk past, my back to him.

"Morning, wife." I can almost hear the fucking smugness in his voice. Jackass. "I've got you a coffee here," he continues as I pull a mug from the cupboard.

"Oh." I put the mug back and finally turn to face him. I see a second cup on the table and make my way over, dropping into the seat opposite him as he pushes the mug towards me.

"Thanks," I say as I take my first sip, savouring the taste.

"I've already taken care of the cleaner and cook, they won't be returning here, so the house is free to do as you please," he informs me, and my eyes go wide.

"You sacked them already?"

"Yes."

"Just like that?"

"Just like that," he confirms.

"But you gave them no warning," I say, shocked that he would take people's livelihoods away at the drop of a hat.

"So?"

"So?" I say, my voice a little high-pitched. "Do you have no heart?"

"I already told you that I don't."

He's got an answer for everything, always ready to defend and conquer. Fuck my life.

"But they had families to look after." I'm not going to let this drop, even though I was the one that said they weren't needed, but still, I don't want to dwell on that too much because the guilt is starting to eat at me already. I've always had compassion, so to see him be so blasé about it really irks me.

"Look, I only did what you wanted, so don't try and make me feel guilty because it won't work," he says, and I feel that little pang of hate start to seep through the cracks of whatever the hell it was I felt last night for this guy.

"You're an ass," I tell him before slamming my coffee on the table. I can't be around him another minute as anger floods my body.

I stand up, my chair screeching across the floor as I push it back.

"Why are you getting so worked up over this?" he says, and I stop as I reach the kitchen doorway.

"Because it's fucking shady," I shout back at him.

"Shady?"

"Yeah. You gave them no warning, no time to get another job—"

"Because you wanted them gone," he interrupts.

"Not like this," I yell, anger fuelling my reaction. "I thought you would give them notice, I thought that maybe you would show a shred of fucking humanity, but I guess I was wrong." That disappointment rushes through me again and I try to stamp it out. I shouldn't be feeling disappointed by his actions, I know what he stands for and who he is. A crime lord with no thought for anyone but himself.

"Who exactly are you mad at here? Me or yourself?" he questions, and it catches me off guard.

"What?" I whisper.

"It seems a little dramatic that you're so pissed about the hired help, so I'm just curious as to what is really bugging you?"

I stare at him, unsure of what to say.

Why am I so pissed off? I didn't know those people, not really, they weren't my friends, they didn't do anything for me to get so annoyed about this.

So the only answer to that question is the man asking it himself. Nate. He's the reason I'm so pissed, but I'm struggling to admit why to myself.

"Never mind, Nate," I say as my shoulders slump and I go back to my bedroom, emotions swirling within me.

He said he wanted to break me, and I think he might just manage it because I don't even know who the fuck I am anymore.

Nate

Her reactions confuse the hell out of me. I have no idea what to do with what just happened because until she admits that I'm under her skin, all I can do is push and push to get her to the answer that she needs. She's scared to admit that she feels something for me, it's plainly fucking obvious, and I haven't even begun to show her my world yet. She may have been here for just over six months now, but I've only ever brought her into my working world once.

And that is what I need to do next.

I don't plan on giving her assignments or any bollocks like that because she is my wife, not some fucking kid that wants to prove themselves to me. But what I am going to show her will be dark enough to see whether she can hack this life with me, and if she can't then she's going to be miserable forever because I meant it when I said I wasn't letting her go.

She's mine.

Only mine.

Last night was incredible. Her body, her curves, her beauty, her fucking taste… I'd like to do it all over again, but I had to see where her head was at this morning. And the answer is, I have no fucking idea because she doesn't either.

The ringing of my mobile phone interrupts my thoughts and I pull it from my pocket, seeing that it is Stefan.

"Good morning, Stefan," I greet him.

"You need to get down here," he says, his voice cold and distant. Immediately my guard goes up.

"I'm on my way," I say, but before I can hang up the phone, he speaks again.

"Don't bring her with you."

I chew that over for a second before asking, "Why not?"

"Because she won't want to see this, Nate. Trust me." He cuts the call and now I'm even more curious to know what has happened.

I move from my seat and quickly go up the stairs to tell Kat that I'm going out. She's in her room, looking as delicious as ever in her gym gear. The way the gym shorts hug her ass and the way the vest top clings to her like a second skin has my mouth salivating, but I have business to attend to, so I don't have time to stand here and picture all the ways in which I would stick my cock in her.

"I'm going to work, I won't be long," I say and all I get back is a "Mmmhmm" from her which pisses me off. I expect words, not a goddamn humming noise. I'll deal with her later though. For now, I need to go and see what is troubling Stefan.

"OH MY FUCKING CHRIST," I say as I walk into the room—my headquarters—and see all of the images splashed across the back wall. There must be over one hundred of them.

"See?" Stefan says as he stands beside me with his arms crossed over his chest. "I told you not to bring her."

I walk closer to the wall, looking at each of the images in turn, feeling my blood boil hotter with each and every one.

"Who the fuck sent these?" I ask, my teeth gritted as I struggle to contain my fury.

"We don't know," Stefan says, and I whirl around, shocked that he hasn't found whoever is responsible yet.

"You don't know?" I say with a raised eyebrow. "How the fuck do you not know?"

"The pictures were already in here when I arrived this morning, already stuck to the wall," he informs me.

"I beg your pardon?" I say, even more fucking shocked.

"Yeah, Nate, this is either the work of someone we know or someone that has inside knowledge of how to get in here."

"Have you checked the fucking cameras?" I question. There are cameras in every room here, except for one room at the back of the house, hidden behind a wall that is filled with bookshelves, or so it would seem. Most of the bookshelves are real, but there is a portion of them that are just models to hide a cleverly constructed door to a room that no one wants to go in if they are my enemy. It's where the magic happens, and I look forward to taking whoever did this in there and teaching them a valuable fucking lesson before I kill them.

"They were all turned off for thirty minutes, allowing whoever did this time to get in unseen, put the pictures on the wall and then fuck off without so much as a trace of whoever did this," he says, looking and sounding grim.

"Who was in charge of the cameras?" I ask, because I leave the organising of shift work up to Stefan. I have more important things to deal with than working out a rota for a fucking camera system, or so I thought.

Stefan pins me with narrowed eyes, and I know what name he is going to say before he speaks.

"Jessica," I say for him, and he nods slowly. "Fuck," I yell as I run my hands through my hair in frustration. "And where is she now?"

"We don't know," Stefan says, looking grimmer than before.

"We don't fucking know," I grumble as I turn back to the pictures and accept the fact that I have a goddamn snake in my crew.

I have never hit a woman, and I never intended to, but seeing these pictures makes me want to grab her by the neck and choke her until I see the life seep away. Makes me sound like an asshole, but Jessica has betrayed me, and she has betrayed my wife.

The images in front of me are of Kat. Some of us together, but mostly just pictures of her, out and about, at the house, in the garden, getting into her car, food shopping, the list goes on. Someone is following her, watching her, and I don't fucking like it one little bit.

It took me a long fucking time to trust Jessica, but eventually she proved herself and I thought that having a woman on my team would make some situations easier to handle. Guess I was fucking wrong because it looks like this bitch bided her time to come after me and be a goddamn threat.

A threat to my wife, to her privacy.

A threat to us and to what we might become.

A threat doesn't bother me, I'm used to them, but it bothers me that these pictures are of Kat with a clear intention behind them.

She's going to go off when I tell her, because I have to tell her, she needs to know, and I need to get the fuck home because I've left her by herself, and clearly, she isn't safe.

"Do some digging," I say to Stefan as I turn and make my way from the room.

"Already on it, boss," I hear him say as I go into the hallway and head for the front door, the words on the post-it note in the middle of all the pictures at the forefront of my mind.

Clocks ticking, asshole.
Enjoy your time with her because you never know when it might be taken away.

Chapter Twelve

Kat

MY FEET HIT the treadmill as I run to try and relieve some of the frustration that I feel, but it's not working. I've been at it for the last twenty minutes, and although I can feel the burn in my lungs, it's doing nothing to ease the tension in my body. Usually, a good workout session helps wonders, clears the mind, allows me to think a little more clearly, but today it's not happening, and it's all because of Nate fucking Knowles.

The guy won't leave my mind, and all I keep doing is picturing him on top of me, his lips pleasuring me, his body moulding with mine. I was hoping that a fuck would help to alleviate my emotions, help to just get over the fact that I hate Nate but wanted to fuck him at the same time... but all it has done is make it worse. I don't just want one night with him; I want another and another, because damn, I have never felt what I did with him. He knew how to trigger my body, how to pull every single ounce of pleasure from me, and he did it all without really knowing me.

I may be married to him now, but I've never let him in. I've never shown him the real me because I had no desire to before...

but I feel different now. I feel like we could be something special, and I despise that I feel this way. I'm struggling. I'm drowning. I don't know what to fucking do.

I have no one to speak to, no one to confide in, no one to unload my problems on. All I have is a house full of expensive shit that I don't really need, and my mind at constant war with my heart.

I want him. I don't want him.

I hate him. I don't hate him.

I could fall for him. I really don't want to fall for him.

Argh. It's killing me slowly, one day at a time, but I've always been stubborn, and I need more than the beauty of his lips and cock to make me see that this could be something.

The gym door opens, and there he is, standing in the doorway looking fucking edible. See? I have no rational thoughts around him. It goes from cold to red fucking hot within seconds, and I can already feel my pussy tingling in anticipation.

I know he is a dangerous man, but maybe that's what I want? Danger. A little uncertainty. A life where I'm always living on the edge but with a man who will never let me down.

I continue to run even as he makes his way into the room, our eyes locked on one another, the music blaring out around us because when you have a private gym, there's no need for headphones.

He comes to stand in front of the treadmill, his hands in his trouser pockets. "We need to talk," he says loudly, so I can hear him over the beat of the music.

"I'll be done in twenty minutes," I tell him.

"Now, Kat," he says, his eyes boring into mine.

I roll my eyes as he reaches over the front of the treadmill and decreases my speed until I come to a stop. Trying to regain my breath, I put my hands on my hips because I am pissed off he thinks he can come in here and just end my session because he wants to fucking talk to me.

"I told you that I would be done in twenty minutes," I grit out.

"And I told you that I need to talk right fucking now," he retorts.

"Argh," I say as I throw my hands in the air and get off of the treadmill, grabbing my towel and wiping my face down. "And what is so important that it couldn't wait until I was done? Because I've been pretty fucking irrelevant up until now, Nate, so what's changed?" I shout, my chest heaving as I try to control myself.

"Fucking mouth," he mutters. "Something happened and I need to talk to you about it."

"Why?"

"Meet me upstairs and I'll tell you."

He goes to walk out of the gym, but I step into his path, stopping him.

"No. Tell me now," I say, determination coursing through me, my body coming alive at his close proximity.

"Christ's sake, do you always have to be so fucking stubborn?" he says, and I smirk because I seem to enjoy pissing him off.

"Do you?" I say, throwing his question back at him. I see the fire blaze in his eyes, and he steps forward, his hands moving out of his pockets and coming to rest on my hips as he walks us backwards until I hit the wall. My heart races as he looks at me, and then he moves forwards, resting his forehead against mine.

"Kat, I need you to listen to me, and I need you to trust me," he says, and the urgency in his voice has my attention. "I need you to know that you are safe with me. I will protect you and I will fucking gut anyone that tries to come near you."

I gulp at his words, suddenly feeling like this took a turn that I wasn't expecting.

"Do you believe me?" he asks, and I see the desperation for me to say yes. I see it inside of him, his eyes giving away what he is feeling in this moment. I see the want, the need, the way in which he goes from cold-as-fuck to panty-melting in a heartbeat.

"Yes," I whisper, and I swear to God that he can hear my heart thumping.

"Okay," he says before delivering news that absolutely has me fucking scared. "Someone is following you, Kat. Pictures were left at my headquarters of you doing normal errands, in the garden, walking down the street, going to functions with me…" His voice trails off and I stare at him in shock.

"What?" I whisper as my hand comes up to cover my mouth.

"Someone managed to get into my headquarters with these pictures, and I promise you that I will find out how and why," he continues, but I'm still stuck on someone following me.

"Someone's following me?" I whisper as my eyes fill with unshed tears and I start to shake.

"Hey," he says quietly as his hands cup either side of my face so I am looking at him. He bends down slightly, so that we're eye level. "I promise that no one will hurt you."

"Is this real? Are you trying to fuck with me right now?"

"No," he answers with no hesitation. "I would never fuck with your safety, Kat."

"Do you know who it is?" I ask, my voice still a whisper because I'm struggling to make myself louder.

"Not yet," he grits out, seemingly pissed off that he can't answer me.

"Is it because I married you?" I ask, almost afraid of what the answer to that is because I know damn well that I wasn't being followed before. I mean, how does he know that I haven't been followed for the whole of the last six months? And how has no one noticed? How have I not noticed? *Probably because you've been too busy fantasising about fucking your husband, Kat.*

"I don't know," he replies, and I push his hands off of me and move away because if I don't then he's just going to get into my head more—and probably my knickers too because I'm becoming weaker and weaker when it comes to resisting him. Damn my pussy for making me give in to temptation last night.

"You don't fucking know?" I say when I'm a few feet away from him. Distance is good. I need distance. "You mean the great powerful Nate Knowles doesn't know who has been following his wife?"

"Kat—"

"No," I shout. "Don't fucking 'Kat' me." My rage starts to return at the ridiculousness of my life. "I guess it would be different if this were a real marriage, huh? I guess you would already know who stalks your wife, and they would already be serving their punishment. But because this is as fake as the fucking smile on my face, I guess I shouldn't expect anything else.

"And don't you dare come at me with some bullshit about how you're working on it and about how I am totally safe with you, Nate. You took my fucking life and turned it upside down. You made me give up everything that I knew to come and be your goddamn side-piece. I'm totally fucking losing myself being here, and now I get the added stress of watching my back because someone clearly wants to take a shot at me." I heave as I rant, feeling better for expelling some of the anger from my body.

"A bit dramatic, Kat," he says and that pisses me off further. "No one has taken a shot at you—"

"Yet," I interrupt.

He glares at me and I cross my arms over my chest and straighten my back in defiance.

"And no one will fucking shoot you, so there's really no need to panic," he continues, and I scoff. "Now, tell me, what exactly did you leave behind in your old life other than a failed fucking business and an ex-boyfriend who ran at the first sign of trouble?" he questions, and before I can think about it, I'm stood in front of him, my hand slapping his cheek, the sound echoing around the room.

Seconds tick past. Time seems to slow.

And just when I think that I've crossed an unforgivable line by hitting him, his lips connect with mine, and he lifts me so I can wrap my legs around his waist. Nate carries me out of the gym and along the hallway, not stopping until we reach the ensuite in his room. Without missing a fucking beat, he reaches out and turns the shower on before we're frantically ripping each other's clothes off. Once naked, his lips come back to mine as he walks me into the giant walk-in shower, pushing my back against the tile as the hot water cascades over us.

He nudges at my opening, and I slide down on him, crying out as he enters me fully. Dear God, this man's cock is a thing of phenomenal pleasure as he pulls out and enters me over and over again.

"No matter what happens between us, Kat," Nate says, his lips by my ear, his forehead resting against the tiles. "I will always look after you, even when you're hating me, even when you want to run from me. I. Will. Always. Be. There," he promises as he thrusts into me, making me moan out loud, his words pushing me higher.

"One day you'll learn to love me, Kat," he whispers as his thumb pushes against my clit, moving in circles as he pounds into me a little slower, slowing down the pace. The way he speaks with so much emotion has me desperate for everything. I want the relationship of my dreams, I want the guy that will love me more than life itself, I want the kids and the dog running around the garden... I want it all, but is Nate really it? Is he really the one for me? Our circumstances are far from fucking normal, but did this happen for a reason? Was he meant to come into my life?

Can I really have it all with him?

"Nate..." I whisper his name as he moves his thumb a little bit faster, pushing against my clit harder.

"What do you want, Kat?" he says as the pleasure threatens to consume my body completely. "Tell me," he urges, his cock plunging into me a little harder again.

"Oh God," I say on a breath, so close to the release that I need.

"Tell me," he says again as he brings everything to a halt, shocking the hell out of me as every single bit of pleasure is abruptly stopped. I stare at him, and he's there with one eyebrow raised as he waits for my answer.

My heart beats wildly in my chest. Shit. Do or die time, Kat.

"I want you," I whisper, my eyes connected with his. "Even when I hate you, I want you," I admit. "Even when you make me want to run, I feel like I can't go because there's something between us."

Dear God, why am I saying all of these things to him out loud? And even as I think it, I can't stop myself from saying the words that I never thought I would. "You don't need to break me to make me love you, Nate, because I'm pretty sure I'd get there on my own."

And fuck, it's like I've ignited a fire inside of him as he pounds into me, my back hitting the tiles over and over, my fingers digging into his shoulders, his mouth on my nipple, his hands either side of my head as he ferociously takes me. And seconds later, we both find our release at the same time, together, in sync. I scream, he roars. I tremble, he holds me up. And when we've both come back to earth, he washes me whilst kissing me, he dries me before I crawl into his bed, and then he curls around me, pulling me to him, keeping me close.

He moves my hair to one side, placing light kisses on my shoulder and along to my neck before I turn my head and let him place his lips on mine. And this kiss is something more than all of the others. More intimate. More emotional.

We kiss slowly, our tongues stroking gently together, my body turning around so I'm facing him, my leg hooking over his hip because I still don't feel close enough. His hand rests at the top of my thigh, his heat searing through me.

I never expected this. I never asked for this. But I absolutely fucking want it. Right now, I want nothing more.

He was right when he said I had nothing before, and the realisation pissed me off because it was painfully true, but now it seems I have something to fight for, and I don't just mean my life.

Chapter Thirteen

TWO MONTHS AGO

Nate

"COME ON, NATE, EASE UP, BUDDY," my personal trainer says as I
slam my fists into the punch bag. Hit, hit, hit, hit, over and over again until my
knuckles crack and my hands ache from the sheer force of each blow.

I'm fucked off and trying to work out some of the goddamn frustration I feel
for the woman living in my house, sauntering her fine ass around the place day in
and day out, and me not getting to fucking hit it.

Honestly, she just waltzed right into the kitchen this morning, wearing
nothing but one of my shirts. Yes, one of my shirts. She doesn't even sleep in my
bed, but she seems to think it's okay to don one of my shirts around the place,
and she's honestly never looked sexier. So, here I am, hitting the bag with sweat
dripping off of me to work out some of the tension in my body when I picture
my lips on hers, my tongue tracing lines over her body and my cock inside of her
pussy… Argh.

She shows no signs of letting up on her hatred of me, even though I can see
that I intrigue her. She wants to know more but her stubborn ass stops herself
from asking questions I would gladly give answers to.

Four months she's been with me, and she's fought me at every turn. It's a
good job I like a good challenge.

I stop hitting the bag, grabbing my water bottle and drinking it all in one.

"What has gotten into you, man?" Brody asks. "I've been your personal trainer for a long time now, and I've never seen you hit the bag that damn hard."

"It's nothing," I say as I regulate my breathing and wipe the sweat off my brow.

"Oh right," he says. "So, it's got nothing to do with the woman who has been wandering around your house for the last few months?" I look at him to see that he is smirking. Fucker.

"I'm not paying you to be my agony aunt, Brody, so let's just get back to fucking boxing, hmm?" I say as I turn back to the bag and throw my fists into it again.

Kat

Fucking man.

I've gone out of my way to try and piss him off as much as possible, and he's not making a bloody peep about it. This morning, I walked into the kitchen in one of his shirts. I didn't ask to wear it; I just took it from his room and put it on. To be fair, it was soft as hell and smelt of his alluring scent, so it was no hardship, but still, I wanted a reaction from him. Anything to show me that he has humanity, anything to show me there is some emotion there. I just need something.

I'm turning into a whiny twat and I don't like it.

I'm still in his shirt, paired with some black leggings. I don't know why I kept the damn thing on. I'm so mad at myself for playing these ridiculous games with him. I need to get a grip and find myself again because all I'm doing is losing who I am around him.

"Get changed, we're going out," he barks from behind me, making me jump. My eyes lock onto his bare back as he marches up the stairs and disappears from view.

"Going where?" I shout as I make my way up the stairs.

"Out," he shouts back.

I roll my eyes at his vague answer and enter my bedroom. I don't want to go anywhere, but then I guess it beats sitting around here for yet another day doing nothing. I quickly grab some skin-tight jeans and a cream V-neck top, pairing it with my killer boots. I leave my hair down, hanging in loose waves, and I do my make-up a little more dramatic than usual, making my eye-shadow darker and my lips a deep red.

I survey myself once in the full-length mirror, and even I can see that I look fucking hot. With a smile, I walk out of my bedroom and bump into Nate in the hallway. Literally, I walk smack bang into his chest.

Oh damn. I lick my lips as I look him up and down and see that he is wearing his black trousers, grey shirt and black tie, which just so happens to be my favourite suit of his.

"Watch where you're going," he says before walking down the hallway, leaving me with my mouth open and my irritation ramping up a notch.

I follow him outside and to the car, getting in the passenger side as he gets in the driver seat.

"Are we going to be out for long?" I ask as he starts to pull off the driveway.

"I'm not sure."

"Are we going out for lunch or something?"

"No."

"Shopping?"

"No."

Jesus, he's not going to give anything away, is he?

"Come on, Nate, just tell me where we're headed," I say, trying once more.

He turns to me with a smirk. "You're about to get your introduction to my world." And with that, he turns back to the road and drives at speed.

Well, okay then.

WE PULL up to a rundown building, and I immediately clock the three SUVs parked outside, two men stood by the side of each one.

Nate pulls us up alongside the cars and gets out, coming round to my side of the car and opening the door.

He holds his hand out for me to take. "Jeez, such a gentleman," I say sarcastically as I comply and get out, steadying myself once I'm standing.

"Now is not the time for your quick wit, my love," he says before closing the

car door and turning to me. "You are about to see what kind of man I can really be."

I don't get a chance to say anything as he takes my hand and leads me to the other cars, and it is at this point that I notice Stefan is one of the men waiting.

"Stefan," Nate greets before nodding to the other guys.

"Nate. Kat," Stefan says, turning to me and smiling. I smile back and admire the fact that he is good-looking. Cropped light-brown hair, deep green eyes, stocky frame and a goatee that is shaped perfectly. He doesn't have a patch on Nate's looks, but it's safe to say that most of these men are pretty easy on the eye. I'm sure there would be a queue of women just waiting to take my place and open their legs for any one of these guys...

"Kat," Nate says as he gives my hand a little squeeze, gaining my attention.

"Yeah?" I say, turning to him.

"We're going in. You will stay with Stefan as a spectator. You are not to say or do anything. You are merely getting a look at the man you are marrying in action."

"Duly noted," I reply dryly, and I hear one of the guy's chuckle before quickly composing themselves.

"Good," Nate says before turning his attention to the men. "If anything goes wrong and anyone attempts to get near Kat, you are to make sure that you take whoever it is down. I do not care for anyone thinking that they can touch or get near my fiancée, is that clear?" he tells his guys, and they all nod their heads and say, "Yes, boss." It's clearly not their first rodeo.

I gulp as we walk towards the building with its chipping paintwork and graffiti sprayed in several places. It looks deserted, no one in sight, but as we near a door, I can hear the sounds of voices.

Nate turns to me and puts his finger over his lips to warn me to stay quiet. I nod my head and then he opens the door, walking in as if he owns the place, the voices dying down as they all turn to look at him, one by one.

"Good evening," Nate says as he lets go of my hand and I feel Stefan drop beside me, his hand coming in front of me to halt me. This is clearly as far into the building as I go. Nate keeps walking into the middle of the room, and I count five men. Five to our six, so at least we're one up on them.

"It's come to my attention that you're late with our payment deal, again," Nate continues, his gaze zeroing in on a guy sat to the left of him. "So, you want to clue me in here, Eugene?" he says, his arms going out wide either side of him.

"We hit a bit of a snag," this guy—who I presume is Eugene—says. "We can't get the money to you until next week."

"Ah," Nate says as he bobs his head up and down. "Next week. Well, why didn't you say so?" He laughs, but I know it's not genuine. I can hear the underlying threat in his tone, but clearly this Eugene is too fucking stupid to see the same as me.

Eugene looks to his other guys and they all join in the laughter, their shoulders instantly relaxing which is a foolish move if ever I've seen one.

"I knew you'd be cool about it," Eugene says as he gets off of his seat and goes towards Nate, clapping him on the shoulder. I watch as Nate's head turns to the side and his eyes land on Eugene's fingers.

And then his face changes.

His eyes darken, his jaw tenses, and before I know what is happening, Nate has Eugene's hand spread out on a table to the right of him and he pulls a knife from his pocket. Eugene starts to shout, as do his men—or whoever they are. Nate ignores it all as he brings the knife down, holding it above one of Eugene's fingers.

"I don't appreciate being fucking lied to, Eugene, so just pay up and I'll be on my way," Nate grits out, and I can see the knife is a whisker away from Eugene's skin.

"I'm not lying, Nate, please, I need more time—" His words are cut off as Nate's patience wears thin and he cuts Eugene's finger off, slicing it as if it were no effort at all. Eugene's men all stand up, some of them knocking their chairs over behind them as they stare aghast at the finger that has been separated from Eugene's hand. Eugene has gone a shade of grey as he looks to his hand in shock.

"Now, I've shown enough patience with you, and I don't have much more to give. So just hand over my money and this ends," Nate says, cool as a cucumber. Just another day at the office, clearly.

"Get the money," Eugene manages to say as one of the guys goes to some cupboard which is hidden behind a dirty as fuck blanket. He pulls a wad of cash out and starts to walk over to Nate, but Stefan beckons one of Nate's other guys over and he takes the cash from the guy, counting it to make sure the payment is all there.

"One month here, boss," he informs Nate, and Nate lets out a fake as fuck chuckle.

"Not enough," Nate says as he gets another of Eugene's fingers and slices it *clean off. Eugene squeals and I can't take my eyes off of what is happening in front of me.*

This is the man I am marrying.

This man is going to be my husband, and I have to be okay with this?

"I want the full amount," Nate tells him, and Eugene's panic goes up a few more notches.

"I don't have that kind of mon—" Another finger is sliced off and Eugene howls so loud that it hurts my ears. One of Eugene's guys looks like he's going to be a fucking hero as he moves closer to Nate, but then Nate's men pull their guns out, training one on each guy. Stefan is the only one who doesn't, and I guess that's because he's fucking babysitting me.

"You only have two left on this hand, Eugene, and I've got no problem cutting them from the other hand before moving to your toes because I am not leaving here until I get my money." Nate's threat echoes around the room, and I start to wonder why the fuck he brought me here. I'm not sure what this is supposed to achieve.

"Please, Nate," Eugene begs, but all Nate does is grab another finger and cut it right off. Blood covers the table and I suddenly wish that I were anywhere but here.

"Only one left, Eugene," Nate taunts him, and I see Eugene is struggling to stay upright. To be fair, I'd have probably passed out by now from the sheer fucking pain of it all.

"Last chance before you lose the last one on this hand," Nate says.

"Get him the money," Eugene rasps out between breaths, sweat pouring down his face.

Nate turns to the men behind Eugene and says, "Well, you heard the man, go get my fucking money."

The guy who grabbed the first wad of cash disappears into another room, returning minutes later with a bag which he drops on the floor. One of Nate's guys goes and gets it, unzipping it, and I get a glimpse of the amount of cash inside. I feel like my eyes bug out of my head from the sight of it all. I have no idea how much is there, but Nate's tactics sure worked.

"That wasn't so hard now, was it?" Nate says as he lets go of Eugene's hand and he crashes to the floor, blood starting to drip off the side of the table.

"I never want to see any of your faces again," Nate says as he points the knife to each of them individually. None of them speak, they just stand there,

gobsmacked and trembling as Nate swiftly walks towards me, taking my hand and leading me out of the building. I have to walk fast to keep up with him, and I have never been so grateful to be out of a building in all my life. I get to the car and plonk my ass in the seat, shock taking over my body as I start to tremble from what I just witnessed.

Nate gets in the car and buckles up before turning to me. "You okay?" he asks and I turn to face him, fucking flabbergasted.

"Am I okay? Am I fucking okay?" I say to him, my voice high-pitched. "What the hell was that? Was it supposed to scare me?"

"Not at all. I just thought that you needed to see some of what I do and trust me when I tell you that was tame. I wouldn't usually deal with shit like that, but I didn't want to throw you in the deep end," he says, so blasé about it all. He reaches over and takes my hands in his before continuing to speak. "You never have to be scared of me, Kat, but everyone else does. I would never hurt you; I just need you to know that."

"Right…" My voice trails off because I really don't know what to say.

"I just… I told you that I have a darkness inside of me, and if you are ever going to accept me then you have to accept every part of me."

His words hit me deep, and as he lets go of my hands, faces forwards and starts to drive, I have a million emotions going through me, but the one that stands out above all else is how turned on I was by the power he exuded in there. Isn't that fucked up? Out of everything, I pick out that Nate looked hot as fuck as he commanded the place and chopped some guy's fingers off.

Fuck. I think I'm going to be in deep shit by the time he's done with me, because he's changing how I think already, and I have no idea how to process that.

Chapter Fourteen

Nate

I WAKE up to feel Kat led against me, her head in the crook of my shoulder and her arm across my chest. She's breathing lightly, so I presume that she is still asleep.

Something has changed dramatically between us during the course of the last twenty-four hours. There has been a shift, almost like an acceptance of the fact that she hates me but wants me. Or maybe she doesn't completely hate me anymore?

Her words come back to me... *"You don't need to break me to make me love you, Nate, because I'm pretty sure I'd get there on my own."*

The minute those words left her mouth, it was like something inside of me came to life, a part of me that had been dormant for as long as I could remember. No woman has ever made me feel what I do for her. No woman has ever managed to make a crack in the exterior around my heart. I've never let myself get too close, but Kat is different, and I knew that the very first time I laid eyes on her. I knew I wanted her, knew I had to have her, knew she was different, knew she would be more. So much more.

Certain people can walk into a room and light it up without

doing anything, and Kat is one of those people. Her smile, her eyes, her beauty and her sass makes the room come to life, and in doing so, it's setting me alight. I've always been a hard-faced asshole because I know that people are waiting to fuck you over at the first chance. I mean, trust doesn't come easy, and love is something you should rarely give because it should only be for the most privileged.

I could love Kat.

And that scares the fucking life out of me.

I've never loved anyone before, but I feel this pull inside of me when it comes to her. I have this need to make her smile, keep her safe, piss her off and make her mad at me, because if she feels all of these emotions because of me, then surely, she feels something too?

She stirs and I watch as her eyes flutter open. So beautiful.

"Good morning," I say as her head tilts back and her eyes meet mine, a slight blush appearing on her cheeks.

"Morning," she replies, her voice still sleepy.

"Sleep well?"

"Yeah. You?"

"Never better," I reply honestly. I'm not usually one for lots of sleep, and I'm always up before the birds start singing, but last night, I slept like a log, and I have every suspicion that's to do with her.

I expect her to try and move away from me, but she doesn't. Instead, she slides her hand up my chest, her fingers tickling my skin as they move to the back of my neck and stop at the nape as she allows them to tangle with my hair.

"Nate, what are we doing?" she asks me, and fuck if she doesn't look completely vulnerable as she asks that question.

"What do you mean?" I need to make sure we're on the same page here and that I'm not about to go and show her my softer side and then get fucking burnt.

"What is this? What is happening with us?" Her voice is quiet, like she's shy to ask in the first place.

I move so that I shuffle down the bed slightly until I am eye level with her. I bring her leg up and over my hip, hooking her around me.

"I think this is us learning to like each other," I say, keeping it light because I don't want a deep discussion to turn into something that may ruin what we have right now. I move towards her and place a kiss on her lips and circle my fingers on the outside of her thigh. Goosebumps immediately appear underneath my touch, and I love how I affect her like this. We've only slept together twice and both times have been phenomenal, and her body has reacted to me in a way that tells me that we do belong together.

I move my lips from hers and trail them along her cheek, down her neck and to her shoulder as I move my fingers to the inside of her thigh, circling, teasing. It may only be six in the morning, but I am fucking hungry, and I need to eat now. I continue to make my way down her body, my lips moving over her breast, my tongue flicking her nipple gently. She gasps, arching her back, pushing her front against me.

She wants this, and I'm going to fucking take it.

I move down further and push her onto her back. She widens her legs as I settle between them, my tongue finally getting a taste of her sweet pussy. She's already wet for me and fuck does that turn me on.

I start slowly, gently working her into a frenzy as I lick, suck and swirl my tongue around her clit. I bring one hand up to tweak her nipple whilst the other grips her hip.

"Nate," I hear her say, and I can hear the desire in her voice, so I turn up the pressure. I press my tongue harder, moving it quicker, and then I move my hand from her hip, bringing it down and plunging two fingers inside of her. She cries out, her legs lifting up slightly, sinking onto me as much as possible.

Fuck, I need my cock inside of her.

I move quicker, working her towards release, my lips clamped around her, my tongue working double-time as I hear her breathing fasten, and then she comes—hard—her body trembling.

I quickly move up her body until I am over her and my dick is thrusting inside of her. Her hands grip my shoulders as I pound into her, giving us both a glorious wake-up call.

She feels incredible, and I savour every single second as she moans, writhes and tightens around me. I fuck her furiously, relentlessly, until we are both panting, moaning and free-falling through our combined orgasms.

"Jesus," she says on a breath as I collapse on top of her, totally satisfied and needing more at the same time. It's like I can't get enough of her, not now she has let me in somewhat, and I don't intend on ever giving it up.

I've never wanted to fight for someone as much as I do her. It's like I feel some sense of completeness with her beside me, under me, in my bed and slowly working her way into my heart.

"I need to pee," she says, and I chuckle into the crook of her neck.

"Way to ruin the moment," I tease her as I roll off and let her get out of the bed.

"Not everything is perfect, Nate, you should know that by now," she says as she saunters her delicious ass into the ensuite.

Her words give me food for thought.

Not everything is perfect, but she is for me, and she makes me want to be the man she deserves.

Kat

Christ. If he keeps this up, I'm not going to be able to walk by the end of the week.

I don't know what to think, I don't know what has shifted between us, but something has, and I can already feel my heart opening up to my husband.

I run the tap and splash some cold water on my face before looking at my reflection in the mirror—and I mean really looking. My cheeks are flushed, my hair is messed up, and my eyes sparkle. Actually fucking sparkle. They no longer look dead but full of life, and it absolutely terrifies me.

How can a man who is so dark and depraved make my heart flutter?

How can a man who is so dangerous be so different with me when he needs to be?

And how can a man who takes pleasure in hurting others make me wet for him?

I need to focus on the hate that has consumed me for months rather than the way he makes my pussy tingle and my heart race.

I can't be with someone who acts the way he does... can I?

I'm already married to him; I'm not going anywhere... unless I can find that escape route.

Do I still want to find that escape?

Do I want to be apart from him and live a life where he is just a distant memory?

Gah. The questions play on a loop in my mind, and I have absolutely no idea of the goddamn answers.

"I think this is us learning to like each other."

His words from just moments ago.

Like each other.

Shit.

I need to stick to my original plan of getting out of here.

I need to find peace.

I need to find my happy place.

But what if this *is* my happy place?

What if he *is* my peace?

I shake my head at myself in the mirror.

Nope. Nuh uh. I refuse to believe that a man who cut someone else's fingers off without breaking a sweat is the man for me.

Clark was the kind of man for me until he decided to leave me hanging and take off to save his own ass. Before that, he was sweet, kind, caring to an extent, and he never made me doubt being with him.

Really, Kat? You're gonna pick that loser as someone you want to be with? He ran out on you, and now you have a man who would literally kill for you, who makes you scream his name as he makes you come, who looks at you with pure fire in his eyes, and you wanna try and justify Clark as the man of your dreams?

"Fuck off," I tell my subconscious.

My mind is a motherfucking mess, and now I have to walk back out there and act like Nate doesn't affect me.

I don't want him to affect me, but I do.

I don't want him to want me, but I do.

I don't want to fall in love with him, but I fear that I will.

Jesus.

"Come on, Kat, get it together," I whisper to myself as I take one last look in the mirror, fix myself with some steely determination and grab the robe off the back of the bathroom door, putting it on and wrapping it tight—like the walls around my heart.

With a deep breath, I open the door and my eyes lock on the monster in my bed, and fuck if my steely determination doesn't waver.

He's glorious. Magnificent.

He's looking right at me, his eyes blazing.

Shit.

Those eyes are pools of green that I could get lost in and forget my own fucking name. And this is the problem. He trapped me, made me marry him, told me I would die if I didn't, and now he's making me want to fall for him. I can't. I won't. I…

"Nate," I hear a woman call out, and my eyes widen at the sudden intrusion… and the female voice.

"Oh fucking hell," he says as he drops his head back on the pillow with a sigh before he sits up and rakes his hands through his hair. Christ, the definition of sexy bedhead was surely made up by him because oh my lord, my mouth just watered ever-so-slightly.

He gets up and pulls on his joggers from last night. Grey joggers. Always had a thing for a man in grey joggers, and I'm so fucked it's unreal.

He prowls over to me, a predatory look in his gaze which has my pussy waking up and hoping for round… three? Four?

He stops in front of me, and I have to tilt my head to look at him. He brings his hand to my face, his fingers cupping my chin and then grabbing my cheeks as he pushes me back against the wall.

"You may want to get dressed because we clearly have company," he growls out before he moves his mouth to ear and whispers,

"But stay out of your head, Kat, because I can already see the doubts swirling around."

He moves back until his eyes are level with mine. "And you are mine. No question. No doubt."

He places a light kiss on the end of my nose and then moves away from me, walking over to the door and opening it before pausing and looking back at me over his shoulder.

"And I always get what I want," he finishes before he disappears and shuts the door behind him.

I let out the breath that I had been holding and try to calm down my racing heart.

"Asshole," I grit out as I stomp across the room. He really is so fucking sure of himself, and it fuels the damn irritation inside of me once again. Good. I need to be irritated by him because then I remember what he did and who he is.

A monster.

A crime lord.

And I have no place in my heart for a man that dangerous.

Chapter Fifteen

Nate

"BIG BRO," Zoey says when I get to the bottom of the stairs to see her waiting.

"Zoey," I say with a nod of my head as I carry on past her and go through to the kitchen, clicking the coffee machine on because I feel I'm going to need several caffeine hits today. "To what do I owe the pleasure?"

"Well," she starts as she drops her bag on the kitchen island and hops up on one of the stools. "Seeing as you ran away from your own wedding so quickly and seeing as you blocked my invite to dinner the other night, I thought I would just pop by on the off chance that my brother would actually see me and spend more than five minutes in my company," she finishes, finally taking a breath.

"I did not block your invite because I didn't invite you. You invited yourself," I say as I narrow my eyes on her.

"Exactly," she exclaims, looking at me like I've lost my damn mind. "You didn't even think to invite me, your sister, your flesh and blood, to have dinner with you and your new wife, who—by the way—I barely fucking know because you haven't given me the chance to say more than two words to her." Great, she's on one of her rants. Marvellous. Just what I need as part of my post-sex morning high… not.

I sigh and turn to the coffee machine, busying myself with making us each a cup of the strong stuff. I inhale the smell of the coffee beans as Zoey continues to rant behind me.

I get it, she wants to be involved, but I didn't want her to get close to Kat until Kat felt comfortable, until she started to like me, or even love me… but I guess that plan is out of the fucking window now that Zoey has shown up here to throw her toys out of the pram.

I pick up the cups and turn to see the woman of my goddamn dreams walking into the kitchen. She holds her head high, her chin raised a little, her eyes shooting me daggers. I momentarily frown at her, because why the fuck is she looking at me like that? Then it becomes clear when her eyes drift to the back of Zoey. She hasn't realised this is my sister because all she can see is the back of her and she barely knows her. The thought that Kat might be a little jealous has me smirking in response.

Kat rolls her eyes and then makes her way to the island as I place mine and Zoey's cups down. She walks past Zoey and takes a seat to the side of her, and only then does she let herself look at Zoey, and I see it register on her face that it is my sister and not some other woman like she thought.

"Oh," Kat says as her eyes soften a little.

Zoey's eyes light up and I know that there will be no getting rid of her now. Not that I want to get rid of her, she's my little sister and I would do anything for her, but I was kind of hoping to break down Kat's walls even more, but I guess that will have to wait for the time being.

"Kat," Zoey says excitedly as she takes the coffee I offer her, practically bouncing in her bloody seat. "It's so good to see you again."

I watch as Zoey looks at the woman I am married to in awe—probably because this woman married me. My sister is six years younger than me, and at thirty-one, I've always looked out for her—

something she has come to love and hate in the past. We're usually close, but with me cutting her off of knowing anything about Kat until the wedding invite turned up on her doorstep—two days before the wedding so I could avoid all the questions—has probably hurt her a little bit. The thought of hurting my baby sister makes me feel like shit, but Kat is my business and no one else's... or she was.

"So, how is it being married to the big bad wolf of the crime world?" Zoey says as she picks up her cup and sips her coffee, hiding her smirk behind the rim of the cup.

I roll my eyes and go back to the coffee machine to make Kat a drink.

"Oh, you know, it's um... pretty boring actually," Kat says, and I spin around to face her. She's smirking and Zoey is doing nothing to hide the fucking chuckle coming from her mouth.

"Boring?" I question.

"Yeah," Kat replies with a shrug of her shoulders.

"Boring how?"

"You keep me locked away in this over-sized mansion, I've got nothing to do all day, and you come and go as you please whilst I'm holed up here, bored," she says, and I feel my whole body go tense.

"Why are you keeping her locked away here?" Zoey asks me, and fuck my life, here we go. I'm going to need a damn good reason so my sister doesn't get on my goddamn case about keeping Kat here for no reason at all... except I do have a good reason, which Kat has clearly forgotten.

"Because there's someone tailing her," I tell Zoey before turning back to the coffee machine to finish making Kat's drink.

"Shit," I hear Zoey say. Yes, shit indeed. And I'm not about to divulge all the other reasons I keep my wife here, because Zoey would have a fucking fit if she knew how I had accosted my new bride and I have no desire to deal with that kind of family drama. She may be part of this world, but Zoey still has a heart, remorse, and she feels every emotion, so I will refrain from provoking her wrath for today, thank you very much.

I take Kat's cup over to her, standing beside her and placing it in front of her, my hand briefly resting on top of hers on the table before she takes a breath and pulls it away from me, wrapping both of her hands around the coffee cup.

"Do you know who yet?" Zoey asks me, and I shake my head with a grimace as I sit down next to Kat, making sure my thigh brushes against hers. I don't fail to notice that she squeezes her legs together, and it makes me have some kind of fucking hope that I really do affect her as she affects me.

"Well, I'd like to get to know you better, Kat, so what about you coming and helping me at the club a couple of nights a week?" Zoey says, and I fix my sister with my stare.

"Absolutely fucking not," I reply before Kat can utter a word.

"And why not?" Zoey retorts.

"Because I said no."

"Pfft, you think that shit is gonna work on me? Think again, bro," she says with a scoff, and I see Kat grin out of the corner of my eye.

Give me fucking strength.

"She's not leaving my side," I say as I clench my jaw.

"And what exactly do you think is going to happen, hmm?" Zoey continues, not giving up—as I knew she wouldn't. "There are God knows how many security, there's always at least six of your men prowling inside the place, and I'm there goddammit, or did you forget that you taught me how to slit someone's throat?"

Huh. Well. Fuck. Maybe I got my baby sister wrong with the feeling remorse and all that shit. I haven't really seen her much over the last six months, what with the whole Kat thing going on. I guess I missed something, because now that I look at her properly, there's a new glint in her eye, a determination, and something else that I can't quite put my finger on…

"You want a night off from this asshole, don't you, Kat?" Zoey says with a smirk on her face. If she wasn't my bloody sister, I swear I would have thrown her out of here by now, and she damn well knows it.

"Hell yes," Kat replies, making my sister burst out into laughter.

"Pissing you off already, is he?" Zoey asks.

"You have no idea."

"Fuck's sake, I am sat right here, you know?" I interrupt, to which they both reply in unison with, "We know."

Oh my God, they're going to be like two peas in a goddamn pod. Ordinarily, that would thrill me, but with Kat not fully on my side yet, I have no idea how this is going to play out. I shouldn't give a fuck, and to anyone else, I wouldn't, but when it's my sister, I care. I don't want my sister's view of me tarnished. She accepts this world, this life, what I do, but she separates that from the brother she sees before her. She knows I have a role to play here, one I took on after our father died, so she gets it, and she loves me regardless. But would she still love me if she knew I had threatened Kat with her life in order to marry me? I'm not willing to take that chance.

"So, how about tonight?" Zoey says to Kat, and I watch as Kat's eyes sparkle.

"No," I say before Kat can answer.

"Stop it, Nate, I can speak for myself," Kat says as she turns and narrows her gaze on me.

"You're not going," I say quietly, deadly, so that she knows that she is on dangerous ground.

"You may be my husband but you're not my fucking keeper," she growls, and damn if it doesn't make my dick twitch.

"Watch it," I warn her, but she just smirks. "Fine," I say as I turn away from her and fix my eyes back on Zoey.

"Great, I'll pick you up at six," Zoey says excitedly.

"No need. I'll be driving," I tell them both with a smile.

"Nate, no," Zoey says, but I ignore her.

"Either I go or neither of us do," I respond, feeling all kinds of smug.

"Christ, why are you so bloody difficult?" Zoey moans, but I don't care to answer. I'm difficult because I can be, and until I am sure that Kat isn't in any grave danger from whoever is watching her, I will be going where she goes and vice versa—and maybe even after that because I am nothing if not a possessive bastard when I want to be.

"It's fine," Kat says with a wave of her hand and defeat in her voice. "He's not going to change his mind. It was a nice thought though, Zoey, thank you." Kat stands from her stool and makes her way across the kitchen. "It was nice seeing you, Zoey," she says before she disappears from sight—and I presume goes to another room rather than hanging around in the hallway.

Oh my God, what is that? A lump in my throat? A tightness of my chest? Fuck. No. It can't be. I don't feel guilty... do I?

"Well done, Nate," Zoey scolds me before she gets up and takes her cup over to the sink, throwing it in there with more attitude than is necessary.

"What?" I say as I turn on my stool to face her.

"You know damn well what, big brother of mine." She leans against the worktop and folds her arms. "She's your wife, Nate, not your fucking hostage."

If only she knew.

"We are all we have left, and the fact that you now have someone who you promised to love and cherish should mean that she's allowed to get to know me too. We're family, Nate, and so is she," Zoey says, and fuck if she doesn't make me feel worse. "I know you have control issues, and I know that you protect those that you love, but Jesus Christ, she is still her own person. And I would like to get to know my sister-in-law without you breathing down our necks."

"Why are you pushing so hard for this?" I ask her, because I am genuinely curious.

"Because... I don't have many friends, Nate, and Kat could be the one woman I can spend time with without worrying about what I say or worrying about letting something slip. And as much as you piss me off, I love you, brother, and I want to extend that love to your wife."

Dear God, she's killing me with her words.

"You always did chip away until you got me to crack," I mutter, and I see Zoey smile.

"So, she's coming tonight?"

"Yes."

Zoey squeals and launches herself at me, giving me a hug. "Thank you, Nate."

"I'm still coming with her, but you can be assured that I will be sat in a dark corner, away from both of you, not interfering in the slightest."

"Because of the tail?"

"Yes." And no, but I don't voice that part.

"Okay, I guess I can cope with that, but at some point, you gotta let us just be, Nate. We don't always want men around, you know?"

"Yeah, yeah," I say with a wave of my hand as I get off of the stool and make my way in the direction that Kat did about ten minutes ago. "See yourself out," I say, not looking back.

"Love you, bro."

I hear the happiness in her voice, and it pains me that she has had a life where friends are few and far between. It's not in our nature to trust easily, and we were always taught to be on our guard and never let anyone in unless you are absolutely sure they would take a bullet for you.

The lessons we've learned have been hard but necessary.

And now I have to make sure that Kat keeps our secret and doesn't taint Zoey's life anymore than it already has been.

Chapter Sixteen

Kat

I HATE HIM.

Just when I thought that we were going to get to a place of compromise and me tolerating him, he goes and does that.

Answers for me.

Decides for me.

Control.

I despise it.

I am my own person, and he needs to realise that just because I'm the wife of some crime leader doesn't mean that I don't deserve to live.

Ugh.

Why did I let myself sleep with him, again?

It's muddied everything.

I kind of already like Zoey because she doesn't seem to take any shit from him—and probably doesn't from anyone else either. I feel like she could be an ally in this fucked-up world I have found myself in. But no. He's taken away the one teeny tiny sliver of me having a friend—even if she is his baby sister.

"Asshole," I say angrily to myself before a knock at my bedroom door interrupts me. I turn and stare daggers at it, knowing that it will only be him on the other side. I take deep breaths, wishing he would just fucking leave me alone.

But of course, that isn't going to happen, because the bastard opens the door without being invited in. Another breach of my personal space. Great.

"Come on in, why don't you?" I say sarcastically as I cross my arms over my chest and lift my chin in defiance.

He quietly shuts the door behind him, and I have to wonder why he bothers—seeing as its only us in the house. Or is Zoey still here?

He stands there, his hands in his jogging bottom pockets, his T-shirt moulded to his body, and those sinfully dangerous eyes trained on me. I can't deny that he is fucking fire when it comes to looks, but it takes more than someone's exterior to win me over. It's just a shame I know that he can have his moments, those ones where I see a softer side, where I could easily love him… but the asshole wins out, so I'm good with keeping my distance. There will be no more fucking. There will be no more nice words. There is only room for despising him.

"Kat," he says on a sigh. "Look, you have to understand that you can't just swan off somewhere without things being put in place."

"You mean your men following me like some kind of low-rent bouncers," I retort, and he scoffs.

"Hardly low-rent," he mutters. "Only the best work for me, and I am not going to let whoever is watching you get close, or have you forgotten that there is someone out there who wants to toy with us?"

"Don't you mean, *you?*"

"Probably, but who fucking cares about the specifics?"

"I do!" I say, my voice raised as I struggle to keep a lid on my emotions.

"Don't act like a petulant child, Kat," he scolds me, and I narrow my eyes on him.

"Stop that," I say as I move forward and point a finger in his face. "Don't dismiss me just because you don't like the way I act. Here's news for you, Nate, I don't much like it either, but I am so suppressed, and I feel so trapped that I have no outlet—"

"You want an outlet?" he interrupts, and our eyes bore into each other's.

I can feel that heat building, the tension, the tingling, the anticipation, the fire, the anger, and every goddamn emotion in-between. And this is what fucks me up.

"Come on," he says as he takes hold of my wrist and drags me from my bedroom. I don't try to stop him because what is the point? He's stronger than me and even if I were to try and fight him off, he'll still find a way to make me do what he wants. So, I follow, and even as his fingers grip my wrist tight, I'm not scared of him or where he is taking me.

He takes me down the stairs and through the kitchen, and then out to the back garden. I follow him through the plush surroundings which go on for miles—as do we—until we come to a building that is on the edge of the property, the high walls behind it surrounding the perimeter of his land.

I've seen the building before, but with no windows and a locked door, I have no idea what is in here.

Nate taps in a code and the door unlocks—because of course keys would be too much hassle. He pulls the door open and leads me inside.

The room is dark because of no natural light being let in, and when Nate lets go of my wrist and closes the door, it is pitch fucking black. Good job I'm not afraid of the dark.

I feel Nate behind me, his body close, and I suck in a shaky breath.

I feel his fingers lightly touch my left shoulder before he slowly trails them down my arm, goosebumps left in their wake.

He does the same on the other side before he moves my hair away from my neck, pushing it to one side, and then his breath is feathering over my skin. I have to stop myself from leaning back into him and letting him take me to where my body wants to go.

"Do you feel that?" he whispers, and I close my eyes and grit my teeth together to not give in to all of the urges I have to kiss this man.

"What?" I manage to reply, my voice echoing a little around the room.

"That pull. That rush."

Yes. Fuck yes, I feel it, and I don't want to. But I don't say that. I stay quiet, allowing myself a few moments to relish in having him close whilst we're in the dark, unseen, a stolen moment.

His hands move to my hips and he pulls me back against him whilst holding me firm.

And not for the first time, I find myself wishing that we had met in a different way. That it had been my actual choice to be with him. That we had been able to experience that first meeting, the butter-flies and the nerves.

He trails his lips up my ear and whispers, "Do you trust me, Kat?"

And isn't that the most loaded question I have ever been asked.

Do I?

"Yes," I reply without much hesitation. Because as much as what he did is wrong, I do find myself trusting him. I know that he will protect me. I know that he won't hurt me. And I know that I have to fight daily to keep reminding myself of how he used me to settle a debt.

He could have married anyone, and he chose me, so whilst we're all alone in the dark, I ask him the question that has been bugging me since he walked into my office—with his marry him or die ulti-matum—nearly seven months ago.

"Why me?"

He stills behind me, and my heartbeat kicks up a notch. I don't expect him to answer as the silence stretches on, and I find myself becoming disappointed, but then he startles me by speaking.

"From the moment that you first walked into my office; I knew. I knew that I wanted you, that I wouldn't be able to stop thinking about tasting you, worshipping you and ultimately, making you mine.

"And I knew you would challenge me, make me work and

wouldn't take any shit. So, I saw my opportunity and I took it. I made you my wife, and I will never apologise for that."

His words have me breathing deep. I never expected such honesty, and I know that this is honesty. I've spent enough time with Nate to know when he's bullshitting and when he's being serious.

"How do you know that we wouldn't have worked out if you had just asked me on a date?" I say, needing to keep a clear head even as his scent swirls around me, enticing me, his very presence making me want to crumble like some love-struck fool.

He chuckles quietly and the sound sends shivers running down my spine.

"I don't do dates, Kat. And I never wait for what I want," he says, no apologies in his words.

I get it, he's a man that takes what he wants and doesn't let anything stand in his way, but I'm not an object to be won.

"The thing is, Nate, you can't buy me. I'm not some precious jewel that can be sold to the highest bidder."

"But you are."

"Excuse me?" I say, irritation lacing my tone.

"You are a jewel, Kat, you just don't know it. You're my jewel, and I'll be damned if I am going to let anything change that," he says, and I can't help the sadness that laces my next words.

"But it could have been different. *We* could have been different."

Silence ensues once again, and all of a sudden, he's stepping away from me and bright lights are coming to life, blinding me, making me squint after being in the darkness.

I blink a few times to clear the blurriness, and when the room comes into focus, I see that this is another gym, except this one holds a boxing ring as well as all the boxing equipment you could want.

"You wanna unleash some anger, Kat? Have at it," Nate says as he holds his hands out either side of him.

"And how is this meant to help exactly?" I enquire, because there is a boxing bag in the gym in the house, but it never helps to fully release my pent-up frustration.

Nate smirks and walks over to the ring and gets in. "You wanted to work some stuff out, so come on in here."

"And do what exactly?" I say as I stroll over and climb up the side, joining Nate in the middle.

"There's some gloves in the corner, put them on," he instructs.

"Why?"

"Just do it, Kat."

I roll my eyes and go over to the corner, picking up the pair of gloves that sit there and put them on.

"Okay, so now what?" I ask with a shrug of my shoulders.

"Now, use me." His words steel my breath for a moment.

"Pardon?" Use him? As in… as a punching bag?

"The reason you have all of this aggression is because of me, so I'm giving you a free pass to take a few shots, work it out, and then hopefully we can move the fuck on with our lives without you hating me every goddamn second of every minute of every day."

"This is nuts," I say as I stare at him like he has gone insane.

"Not really. Come on, do your worst," he says, holding his arms out wide, taunting me, egging me on.

"I'm not going to hit you, Nate," I say adamantly as I start to undo one of the gloves with my teeth.

"Do it," he goads.

"No."

"Fucking do it, Kat," he says, his voice louder, pushing me, making me want to scream in frustration.

"Why? What is the fucking point of this?" I say, raising my own voice to the same pitch that he did.

"Because maybe if you take a few swipes at me, just maybe you'll start to fucking see that you don't hate me," he says, taking a step closer.

"That makes absolutely no sense," I argue back, ripping the first glove from my hand and throwing it at his feet.

"It doesn't have to make sense. I just need you to stop being so goddamn hostile."

"Then maybe you shouldn't have fucking kidnapped me," I bite back.

"Kidnapped you? I fucking rescued you!" he shouts, getting in my face.

"And that's your idea of rescuing someone? Marry me or die? And what the hell did I need rescuing from anyway? I had a good life, an honest life—"

"Yeah, so honest and good that you had a boyfriend who sent you to me, who made you come crawling for money before he gambled it all away on shitty poker games and cheap women—"

He doesn't get to say anything else as the rage in me runs so fucking deep that I do what he asked, and I hit him. Right on the goddamn jaw. His head whips to the side before he turns back to me, his hand whipping out and grabbing me around the throat.

And I am anything but terrified as he throws me down and pins me beneath him, his legs straddling me, caging me, his free hand pinning both of mine above my head.

"You tell me that I don't make you feel alive, Kat," he says in my face. "Tell me that I don't give you the best fucking high of your life."

One... Two... Three... "Tell me," he shouts, his eyes blazing, his grip a force to reckoned with, but I don't struggle, and instead I shout back at him.

"YES! Yes you make me feel, Nate, but I also hate that you make me feel because I'm not meant to fucking like you..." My voice trails off as the heat of the moment becomes too much, and then his lips smash down onto mine.

I lose myself in his heat, his warmth, his tongue. It's all so fucking good, and the emotions that he brings out of me are all-consuming.

I hate him.

I like him.

I want him.

I need him away from me.

I have to escape.

I have to stay.

Like a merry-fucking-go-round.

I am a mess, and I am losing myself more and more… or is he making me wake up?

I'm not sure, but as his tongue continues to merge with mine, I know I need to stop this. I need space. Distance. A moment to just fucking think.

"Stop," I whisper against his lips, and he complies immediately, his forehead resting against mine.

"You're not the only one struggling here, Kat," he says, so quietly, so softly, so unlike Nate.

His words cause tears to sting the backs of my eyes, and I feel like I can't breathe properly.

I've had him inside of me, kissing me, touching me, making me come in ways I never knew possible, but right now, I need him to get off of me and leave me be for a while.

"I need to go," I tell him, still whispering, still struggling to breathe.

He moves his head back slightly and looks deep into my eyes, and damn if I don't feel like I can see right inside his soul. A soul that I know is capable of loving me the way I want and how I should be loved.

But I'm scared. Terrified.

And I know I'm falling deeper under his spell despite how I came to be here.

I see his jaw tense before he moves off of me, rising to his full height and holding his hand out for me to take. I do, and I let him pull me up, and then I turn away from him and leave the boxing ring, jumping down and making my way across the floor.

I don't turn around, I stay facing forward, my eyes fixed on the door—all the while feeling his gaze burning into my back.

And when I get outside, I take a deep breath of fresh air and make my way back to the house, where the thoughts keep swirling on a loop in my mind, driving me crazy.

Could I love Nate?

Could I be the wife that he wants me to be?

Could he be the husband that I always envisioned?

And those thoughts alone are the ones that continue to haunt me, because if I can love him despite him being a crime lord, if I can forgive him for making me part of his life in the way that he did, then I know that he will have the power to crush my heart to nothing but dust if this were ever to end.

And I don't know if I would be strong enough to get back up again after.

Chapter Seventeen

Nate

"YOU READY TO GO?" I ask Kat as I peer around her bedroom door.

After she left me earlier, I stayed in the boxing ring and just sat, thinking, wondering what the hell is going on in her head.

I get it, the way we started out wasn't ideal, but fuck, I've shown her softer sides of me that no one has ever seen before. I don't know if I still want to break her apart completely, I don't know if that is still a goal of mine because I am starting to realise that there might not be any point to it.

She has to love me for me.

She has to accept me for me, and at this point, I don't know if she ever will.

The heat is there, that fire that burns between us is like a goddamn inferno that is at risk of spreading like wildfire, but is that enough?

"I'm ready," she says as she comes into view and takes my fucking breath away. She's dressed in a pair of black tailored shorts that come to mid-thigh, a skin-tight white vest top that seems to sparkle against the light when she moves, and a pair of black ankle boots that I would love her to keep on whilst I fucked her into oblivion.

Then there's her hair, sleeked back into a high ponytail and poker straight. Her makeup is heavy, dramatic, and her lips coated in a deep red like they're inviting me to stick my cock in her mouth and have her lipstick marks smeared all over my flesh.

Jesus fucking Christ.

I'm hard already.

I clear my throat, unable to rip my eyes away from my smoking hot wife, and I see her smirk. See? That fire, that playfulness, it's there, so why is it so hard to navigate anything else between us?

"I'll wait downstairs," I tell her before I make myself move, and I swear I hear the faint sound of her chuckling as I do. I can't help but frown as I make my way down the stairs.

Nate Knowles. Big bad wolf. Crime Lord. Shows mercy to no one… except one woman. One woman who he made sure was his. The only woman to have gotten this close to him. And he no longer has any idea how to play this. Fuck my life.

I had a clear-cut plan when I went after Kat. Make her mine, break her, have her need me. Simple. And even though I could see that she would challenge me, I never expected to start to fall for her so fast and so hard. Because that is what is happening here. Cold-hearted killer, falling for a woman who continues to hate him.

I run my hands through my hair, messing it up a little, but I give no fucks. I couldn't care less what people think of me, and as long as they fear me and what I am, then all is golden, so my hairstyle is the least of my fucking worries.

There is only one person whose thoughts I care about, and she's just walked in the room and is standing right in front of me, looking like a goddamn goddess. And then she smiles at me. A gorgeous, no holds barred smile. One I haven't seen before, and fuck… something inside of me stirs… what is this feeling?

"We going?" she says, her eyes twinkling, and the fact that I haven't seen her this—dare I say—happy before has me all kinds of fucked-up inside.

"Sure," I manage to choke out as I mentally give myself a bloody pep talk to stop acting like a teenage boy with a hard-on. I move towards her, and the smile stays on her face, so I take my chances and hold my hand out to her.

She looks, she waits, and if I were a chick, my heart would be skipping a goddamn beat right about now. But then she puts her hand in mine, her fingers linking through mine, and then she looks up at me and there is an innocence about her in this moment. One where I know that I don't want to break the woman before me until she needs me so desperately that she can't be without me. I don't want to break her to get to that point. I want her to want that for herself. I want her to let me in, give me everything, and in return, I will give her the same. Because she has me in her grip. I'm hers whether she realises it or not. And she is mine.

I close my hand around hers and quietly tell her, "You look amazing." Amazing? *Jesus Christ, Nate, could have gone with a better word than that, for fuck's sake.*

"Thank you," she says as I see a blush cover her cheeks. A blush. A goddamn blush. "You don't look too bad yourself." And the compliment almost has my jaw opening in shock—almost. I have had years of schooling my reactions, so I contain the fact that I want to grab her and kiss her, claim her and fuck her into oblivion, as well as containing my shock at her words, obviously.

I lead her from the house and out to the car, opening the passenger door for her so she can get in. My men are already in position, watching, waiting, and they know exactly where we are going. I pay them to protect me and to use whatever means necessary to do that, so it enables me to worry a little less—most of the time. Right now though, I am on fucking pins. Someone we are yet to locate is tailing my wife, so I am on high alert. I didn't want her to go to Zoey's club tonight, but my sister doesn't let things drop easily, so here we are, driving to the club, and damn if I don't want to turn the car around and lock Kat inside the walls of my house—where I know she is safe at all times.

Why the hell did I agree to this?

When do I ever do shit that I don't want to do?

I look to the woman sat beside me, and the answer is obvious.

Because of her.

I'm doing this for her.

We drive in silence, but I keep looking at Kat out of the corner of my eye, and there is a faint smile on her face which makes me feel… happy?

I can't remember the last time a woman made me feel anything close to happiness, but Kat is it. I know she is, even when she pushes me away and tells me she hates me. It doesn't matter because I'm never letting her go anyway.

I drive through the town and come to a stop outside Purity— Zoey's nightclub. The name is so far from what we are that it's laughable.

There is a line of people, waiting to gain entry, but of course, we won't be queueing tonight. I turn the engine off and look to Kat. "You still want to go in?" I ask her, praying that she says no, but I already know that she won't.

"Yeah," she says, her eyes sparkling, a smile on her face and an energy coming from her that I've never felt before.

I blow out a breath and run my hand through my hair before I look at her one last time and then get out of the car, walking around to her side and opening her door and holding my hand out to her. She places her hand in mine and I help her out, stepping close to her when I shut the door. I lower my lips to her ear and breath in her scent as I say, "Don't forget who you belong to tonight." I lick my tongue along the shell of her ear, and I feel her shiver—hopefully with fucking delight.

I don't let her say anything as I take her hand and move us around the car and to the steps that lead to the front doors of the club. I chuck my keys to one of my guys—because this whole place is roaming with men that work for me—so he can go and park it whilst we head inside.

When we do, I hear a few grumbles from the people in the line because Kat and I just walk right past them. But I pause and turn to look at them, a mean as fuck look on my face, and they quickly look like they just shit themselves. I smirk and carry on, walking through the entrance which is large with a seating area to the left and a booth to the right where you pay on entry. We skip that part and head on past the cloak room where people can drop their coats and whatever else they don't want to carry around with them. The lighting in here is dim but bright enough to see what you're doing, the music from the club pumping in the background, the bass vibrating through the floor.

I reach the doors of the main room, the lights flashing through the frosted glass panel before the music hits us full force as I open one of the doors. I walk us through, Kat behind me—still holding my hand.

I see several pairs of eyes turning our way as we move through the people milling around the bar area. Most of them will know who I am, and only the stupid ones will be unaware that I am the motherfucking master, but they soon learn who they are dealing with if they try to get all cocky and shit.

We reach the bar and immediately someone is there, waiting and ready to serve us a drink. They've been taught well.

"I'll just take a diet coke," I tell the bartender who then looks to Kat for her drink order.

"Tequila," she says, and I raise an eyebrow at her.

"Just tequila?" I question.

"And a slice of lemon and salt," she adds on with a smile.

I wave the bartender away and then pull her to me, her chest to mine. "You planning on getting drunk, wife?" I ask her, my lips by her ear so she can hear me over the thump of the music.

"Maybe," she says with a wink, and fuck if I don't like this side of her. Playful, teasing, excited. It's new, and it's actually… nice. There is no tension tonight, no hate, no looks like she wants to kill me… yet. I'm sure it will come, but for now, I'll enjoy seeing my wife this way, learning a little bit more about her.

The bartender returns with our drinks, and I watch as Kat licks the back of her hand before sprinkling some salt and picking up the lemon slice. Even her tongue licking the back of her hand has my dick twitching. Jesus Christ. This woman.

She picks up the tequila with her other hand and looks at me.

"Bottoms up," she says before she licks the salt, downs the shot, sucks the lemon, and signals to the bartender for another one.

Before I can say anything, a shriek comes from my right, and then the force that is my sister smashes into the side of me as she wedges herself between me and Kat, putting her arms around both of us.

"I'm so glad you came." She smiles at me before turning to Kat. "Oh damn, girl, you don't fuck about, do you?" she says as she looks to the empty tequila shot and the one that the bartender is placing in front of Kat. "Terry, grab me three of those and one more for Kat," she instructs, and the bartender—who I now know is called Terry—nods and proceeds to do what Zoey asked. "And why the fuck are you drinking coke?" she asks me, a frown on her face.

"Because I'm not here to get shit-faced," I tell her.

"Ah, come on, Nate, live a little," Zoey says, and I see Kat smirk.

"I live just fine, thank you," I reply, picking up my coke and taking a long glug. A fucking whiskey would go down great right about now, but I need to stay alert, just in case.

"Pfft, if you say so, brother," Zoey says with an eye roll and her and Kat start to laugh. "Now, run along, Kat and I have some dancing to do."

Run along? Who the fuck does she think I am? Some little lap dog?

"Nate, you said you would give us some space so I can get to know my sister-in-law," Zoey grits out, and I feel myself scowl at her. Actually fucking scowl. She's a pain in my ass at times. It's a good job I love her and she's family because I wouldn't tolerate it from anyone else.

"Fine." I pick up my drink and make my way to the corner of the dance floor, sitting on one of the stools and making sure I have ample view of the whole place.

The dance floor is starting to fill up, more people entering the club through the main doors. It's good to see the place thriving, but I prefer the private club I own. It's just more of a sanctuary for me, less public, more intimate, and somewhere where you're not going to get some lager-drinking-twat try to take on the world. When people are in my private club, they know they have to behave, and they wouldn't dream of causing shit on my doorstep. It also helps to have the exclusive membership because then I can veto any fucker I don't want in there. Here, I can't do that, because as much as my men watch over the place, Purity is Zoey's baby, and I promised her a long time ago that I wouldn't interfere with the way she ran things—except for the security, of course.

I see Kat and Zoey move to the black and white check dance floor, where the flashing lights bounce off the white tiles. My eyes are everywhere, until Kat starts to shake her hips and I have to adjust myself in my seat. And I can't take my eyes off of her. She's gorgeous, a picture of beauty, and I'm the one that gets to take her home tonight.

I have to force myself not to go over there when other people dance too close.

I have to force myself not to react when I see men looking at her, appreciating her, watching her. Pisses me off, but I said I would give her this night, and I have no doubt that she can look after herself.

I lose count of the amount of times she gazes my way, and I feel like maybe, just maybe, this could be a turning point for us.

I don't know how much time passes before Kat and Zoey go back to the bar, grab another drink, and then I see Kat walk away, towards the toilets. And again, I have to stop myself following her to make sure nothing happens.

She's okay.

She's in my sister's club.

My men are the security.

She's going to be totally fine.

Chapter Eighteen

Kat

I HAVEN'T HAD this much fun in… forever. It seems I've lived a pretty fucking boring life, and it's taken Nate dragging me from what I knew to make me see that he was right. I wasn't living. I was merely existing, thinking that everything was perfect and that I was happy. But actually, I was far from it.

I have experienced more emotions than ever before since being with Nate, and the hate that I tried to hold onto for so long is slowly seeping away, being replaced by something else. Something I'm not ready to admit yet.

I wash my hands in the sink and turn to face the drier, holding my hands underneath and letting the water droplets run from my fingertips.

My feet are starting to ache from the dancing, but I am nowhere near done yet. If I am being given this night as a 'freebie' of sorts, then I am damn well going to see it through to the end.

Zoey is amazing, like a friend I have never had. Meeting her has been like a breath of fresh air, and although she is my husband's sister, she has assured me that she knows what he's like and that I should take no shit from him.

I hear the door open behind me as I finish up drying my hands and turn back to the mirror for a quick check on my makeup, but the person who has just entered catches my attention from the corner of my eye as I see them reach for the lock on the door and turn it. I slowly turn my head to look at them, and it's not a woman, it's a guy with a fucking snarl on his face... and I'm the only other person in these toilets.

Oh shit.

He looks like a mean fucker. He's about my height, has an athletic build, a bald head, a short beard, and a scar running down the side of his face. His nose looks like it's been broken a few times too. He's clearly no stranger to conflict, and I guess I just became his latest target for whatever fucking reason, I have no idea.

"Uh, you know that this is the ladies', right?" I say, unable to help the sarcasm that drips from my voice. If this asshole is here to try and scare me, then he's going to be disappointed. I live with the biggest monster to walk this earth, so this guy is going to like a pussycat compared to that.

The guy smirks and then charges for me, backing me up to the wall behind me, smashing me against it as his hand comes to my throat and grips tight.

Fucking hell, not even a minute to prepare myself.

"What are you doing?" I manage to choke out as he squeezes his fingers a little more, making it harder to take my next breath.

"Just passing on a little message," he sneers, and his rancid breath hits my nose, making me grimace.

I refuse to act pathetic and try to plead to this guy's good side, because I doubt there is one, so I do the only thing I am able to do whilst he's pinning me to the fucking wall. I lift my arms up and quickly jab both of my thumbs in his eyes, making him yell out and momentarily let go of me.

"You fucking bitch," he shouts, but I don't waste any time as I quickly move around him and run for the door. I am inches away, and as I reach out to grab the door lock, I'm tugged back by my hair. I cry out in pain as it feels like my hair is being ripped from my scalp.

"Get the hell off of me," I say, trying to keep my voice steady, but the panic that I tried to tamp down just seconds ago is rearing its head.

Fuck, fuck, fuck.

I'm slammed back against the wall as if the last few seconds never happened. He slaps me across the face, hard, and then his hand is back around my throat, his other hand gripping my hip.

"Oh, the fun I could have with you," he comments as I try to struggle against him but find myself at a loss as he pushes his chest to mine. I don't even feel the pain in my face because adrenaline is sweeping through me, blocking out the sting. "Hopefully the boss will let me, once I have delivered you to him because I would love nothing more than to fuck Nate Knowles' woman."

Ugh. My skin crawls, and I know if this guy manages to get me out of here then I won't survive. He'll use me for what he wants and then kill my ass. I can see it in his eyes. He's a stone-cold murderer.

"Are you not the boss?" I choke out, trying to buy myself a few minutes to somehow get out of here.

"I will be the fucking boss when my dick is buried inside of you," he replies, and I shudder.

I don't beg for him to let me go because I know he won't, and as he crushes my throat more, I know that I am at very real risk here of blacking out.

Come on, Kat, think.

I try to calm myself in order to think about my next step, and as the guy starts to lift me off the floor, my tiptoes barely touching it, I have a brainwave.

My bag.

Front pocket.

Metal nail file.

Stupid fuck hasn't thought to disable the use of my hands.

I feel woozy, light-headed, but I move my left hand and open the front zip, pushing my fingers inside and feeling for the nail file. It touches the tip of my finger and I grip it, moving it into my hand so

I'm ready to strike. The guy doesn't even notice as he's too busy licking the side of my face, and I take my opportunity.

I bring my hand out of the bag, and with one quick movement, I sink the nail file into the side of his neck, pushing it in as far as it will go. His tongue moves away from my face, his hands falling from me as he stumbles back and lifts one hand to his neck. The blood is already running down his neck, and his eyes are wide with shock.

I don't waste any time as I knee him in the balls and run around him as he drops to the floor like a sack of potatoes. I reach the door and unlock it, my fingers shaky as I pull the door open and come to a halt as I see Nate stood there, four guys behind him, his eyes roaming over me, the worried expression on his face quickly turning to a hardness as his jaw clenches.

But I don't think as I launch myself at him, burying my face in his neck and wrapping my legs around his waist.

I allow my tears to fall, my whole body trembling as I feel him start to move. I don't care where he's taking me, all I know is that I am safe with him.

My one night of freedom has quickly turned into a nightmare.

I hear a door open, and a cool breeze hits my back, but I don't move my head from Nate's neck. I let the tears continue to fall as he carries me, and I feel us sinking lower until he's sat down, me still wrapped around him, a door shutting to the side of us.

"I got you," he whispers, his hand stroking the back of my head. My arms are locked tight around his neck, and I don't think for one minute he is going to ask me to move. He just holds me, letting me drench his skin with my tears.

I don't register anything else other than the feel of him as I try to numb my mind. I don't want to replay what happened tonight, but I know it will come. Maybe I'm in shock? Maybe I'm in denial? Whatever it is, I'll take it because all that matters is that I'm okay in the grand scheme of things.

I feel the car come to a stop sometime later, and then the door clicks open, but still I don't look up. Nate's neck is too inviting for me to want to leave it. He manages to slide out and stand up without asking me to let go of him.

"You know what to do," I hear him mutter—to I presume the driver of the car—and then he's walking, another door opening and closing, and then there is silence except for the sound of his shoes hitting the floor with each step.

We're home. And I know this because the smell of this place hits me. The comforting scent of the house we live in.

The tears are starting to subside as he moves us upstairs until I am being placed on a surface and I finally move my head from the crook of his neck.

I register that we're in a bathroom, but it's not my one. It's Nate's.

My head hangs, my eyes refusing to lift until his hands cup the sides of my face and he tilts my head up.

"Look at me," he says softly, and it hits me right in my goddamn heart. I raise my eyes to look at him, knowing that I probably look a state but not caring at this moment in time.

I watch as his eyes look to my cheek where that asshole slapped me. I watch as his eyes run over my neck, taking in what I assume are red marks from where his fingers were wrapped around me. And I watch as Nate struggles to contain his rage, pushing it back, trying to stay calm.

"Take a shower, and I'll go and make you some sweet tea for the shock," he says before placing a kiss on my forehead. His eyes linger on me before he leaves, closing the door behind him and I let myself fall apart once again. I let the tears run down my face, I let the disgust at having that awful man's hands on me overwhelm me, and I strip my clothes off, turning the shower on and stepping in, scrubbing my skin over and over again. I wash my hair, needing every part of me clean.

I want to be strong; I want to be able to hold my head high, but I feel pathetic right now. Yes, I managed to get away and hurt the person that was trying to hurt me, but at the cost of becoming a possible killer myself?

The realisation that I may have murdered someone makes my legs give way and I drop to the shower floor, bringing my knees up to my chest and hugging them with my arms. How is this my life?

I'm married to the head of the crime world.

I stuck a nail file in a guy's neck tonight.

Does that make me a monster too?

The thoughts assault me, and it isn't until I'm being lifted out of the shower that I register that Nate is holding me again, his clothes drenched as he moves me and places me down, wrapping a towel around me and drying my body.

I let him because I am rendered useless.

I'm not strong.

I'm weak.

I'm not even worthy of being his wife because his wife would be able to deal with this shit, whereas I am just a mess. It's quite a turn-around. I hated him, hated what he made me do, hated how he trapped me, but as he dries my feet, lifting each one carefully, I realise that I don't hate him at all. In fact, I feel my heart flutter as I watch him take care of me. This man who is a monster, tending to me like I am the most fragile thing on earth.

And when his eyes lock with mine, I know that I have fallen.

I've fallen hard and I've been denying it to myself for a while now.

The fire he starts inside of me, the way he drives me crazy, the mindfuck that came from being part of his world, it's all been leading to this moment.

The moment when I know that I am in love with him.

I've seen sides of him that I imagine no one else has.

I've experienced his wrath and his kindness.

I've felt his eyes on me, watching me, assessing me, making me feel like I am his whole world.

And maybe I am, but he deserves more. So much more.

It doesn't fucking matter that he kills.

It doesn't fucking matter that he rules a dangerous world where he cuts people's fingers off when they don't pay up.

None of it fucking matters except for the man who is now standing in front of me, curiosity crossing his face.

I want to be good enough.

I want him to feel like he hit the jackpot when he chose me.

I want it all with him. The house, the kids, the life, the happy ever after.

But the thought has me feeling broken inside. Because I am not that woman. I am not the woman for him. I'm a mess and I've crumbled. Maybe this is my breaking point? Maybe this is what he wanted to do? Break me to make me realise I needed him.

Mission accomplished, except, I don't feel good enough for him.

But for one night, after a shitty way to end what was a few hours of lightness, I am going to allow myself to enjoy the feel of him. The way his hands will caress my body and nothing else will exist. I need it. I need him. I need this one night.

So I say the only words I want to say, pushing the thoughts of doubt to the back of my mind.

"Take me to bed, Nate."

Chapter Nineteen

Nate

IT TAKES me less than a second to pick her up and carry her to my bed.

I lie her down, just admiring her perfect body. Despite the marks on her neck that have a rage bubbling inside of me like nothing else, she is the definition of perfection for me.

Tonight, she showed that she is strong enough to be in my world. She managed to get away and come to me, giving that asshole a bit of retribution in the process. It will be nothing compared to the retribution I will show him, but I don't want to think about that now as I stare at the beauty before me.

I start to strip, undoing my trousers and letting them fall to the floor. Next to go is my shirt, and then my boxers and socks. I stand before her, fully naked and revelling in the way she devours my body and bites her bottom lip.

I lower myself to the bed and crawl over her, until my body covers hers and our eyes are locked together.

Her breath feathers over my lips, her eyes showing how hungry she is for this. For me.

Her hands come up and lightly touch the back of my neck, tracing circles. "Make love to me, Nate," she whispers, and I hear the slight crack in her voice as she speaks. It makes my heart lurch in response. Fucking hell, my heart is hard, cold, black... until her. She's bringing it to life again, and she will be the first woman that I have ever made love to because no one was good enough until she came along.

I dip my head down and kiss the red marks that mar her skin. The handprint on her cheek, the finger marks on her neck. I kiss each one delicately, gently, not wanting to hurt her.

Her fingers move to my hair and run up and down. This isn't going to be rushed, it isn't going to be hard, and it isn't going to be like the other times before.

This is the next step. And I'm about to give her something I've never given anyone before. My heart.

I've kept my heart behind walls of steel, but she's broken through them, and a part of me always guessed that she would be the one to do it. I knew from the very first moment I set eyes on her that she was going to be my end game.

And now here she is. Led beneath me. My wife.

I'm not a sappy fucker, but for her, I'll be what she needs me to be. I'm done playing fucking games and side-stepping what we both know is true. We belong. We are meant to be regardless of how we started out.

I make my way down her body, kissing every inch of skin until I am led between her legs, my mouth in line with her pussy.

I lift my eyes to her, and she's got her head tipped back as she waits for me to touch her. But I want her to see this. I want her to watch as I make her have the most intense orgasm she's ever had in her life.

"Look at me," I growl out, and her head lifts up, her eyes connecting with mine and showing me just how much she wants this.

I lower my lips down and lick her from top to bottom. I repeat the move over and over again, slowly, savouring the taste of her. I'm going to commit every single second of this to my memory and remember it until my dying day.

We both know that we have an intense chemistry anyway, but this is on a whole other level.

I devour her whilst keeping my eyes on her, watching her mouth fall open as I lick, suck and swirl my tongue, making her wetter with each passing second.

I bring two fingers to her opening and slowly move them inside of her as I continue to work her clit, making her open her legs wider, stretching them as far as they will go.

She moans and my dick becomes harder than rock.

"Nate," she says on a whisper as she pants, her breathing speeding up as I increase the pressure on her clit and flick my tongue up and down.

"Oh my God," she says as she continues to watch me bring her to orgasm.

I reach up with my free hand and pinch her nipple, making her groan and her eyes close for a few seconds before they ping back open and collide with mine.

"Shit, Nate, I'm nearly there," she says, and in this instance, I can deal with the swearing because I'm the one making her curse.

"Fuck," she shouts as her legs tremble and she arches her back, her mouth dropping open and her eyes fluttering as she struggles to keep them open. I keep going until I am sure she can take no more—if the writhing around on the bed is anything to go by—and I kiss up her thigh, moving up her body until I am eye level with her again and my cock is at her entrance.

She reaches up and pulls my head down, our lips meeting and her groaning as our tongues merge together. Her legs are now wrapped around me, her feet pushing against my ass and urging me to enter her.

I slowly push my cock inside of her until I am buried deep and we both groan at the feeling. And then I start to move in and out, our tongues still entwining, our lips in sync with one another.

We become one—just like we should have been from the start.

I feel a passion for this woman, a possessiveness, a need.

I've never needed a goddamn thing before her.

Our lips part and my forehead rests against hers as she meets my thrusts. Both of us pant, both of us moan, and both of us come at the same time as we're taken over the edge. And fuck me, it's not just her that's having an intense orgasm, because I feel this on another level too. I roar with my release, and she screams out my name. Sounds fucking beautiful.

And once we've caught our breath, I kiss her again, slowly, sensually. I need her to be feeling what I am feeling right now because if she isn't then I'm going to go insane.

When we finally part, I lie beside her, but I hold her close to me, her leg hooked over my hip, her hands linked behind my neck. She seems to like doing that, and damn, I'm getting to fucking like it too.

I nuzzle my nose against hers as her eyes start to flutter closed and I can see her struggling to stay awake.

"Sleep," I whisper to her, and she holds me a little tighter. Not going to lie, it causes my heart to fucking stop for a beat. Jesus, what is she doing to me?

Her fingers move to the side of my neck and trace the tattoo I have there.

"Does it mean anything?" she asks me, her voice soft.

"No. It's just something I got when I was younger, you know, when you do stupid shit on a whim," I tell her. It was just some design I picked out of a book and had done before I could change my mind.

"It's not stupid... it's part of who you are, and I think it's perfectly you, Nate," she says before she places a kiss on my lips and then nuzzles her head into the crook of my neck.

I listen to her breathing even out, feeling her arms go limp from sleep taking over, and I close my eyes with a smile on my face for the first time in years.

Chapter Twenty

Kat

I WAKE up with my hand led on Nate's chest, his arm around me and my leg swung over the top of his.

I blink a few times to rid myself of the blurriness and I allow myself a few moments to bask in the beauty of what we did last night.

I asked Nate to make love to me, and he did. And it was the most magical experience of my life.

He made me feel like nothing else mattered, like I was his whole world. I've never been made to feel so special, and it's given me food for thought.

I gently disentangle myself from him, careful not to wake him as I crawl out of the bed. I take one of his T-shirts from the chair in the corner of his room and put it on, breathing in his scent and the aftershave he wears.

I take one last look at him and leave his room, making my way downstairs to the kitchen. I start the coffee machine and try to ignore the pain that is searing through my heart at what happened at Purity last night. How that man had his hands on me, how he hurt me, how he made me feel disgusting in every way imaginable. If it hadn't been for Nate, I don't know what I would have been like. He took care of me, made me feel like I mattered, and he ultimately made the hate that I have harboured for him for so long disappear.

I'm done with hating him.

I'm done with fighting against what I feel.

And as much as I dislike the way in which we became a couple, I can finally feel my anger seeping away. I have no idea why that guy attacked me last night, but I presume it was because of who my husband is... and yes, if it wasn't for Nate then that probably wouldn't have happened, but I can't take away from how he looked after me and how when I saw him, I ran straight into his arms, taking comfort from his embrace.

There is no denying that Nate appears to have become my security blanket, and I have mixed emotions about that. I don't want to be someone that depends on a guy for the rest of my life, but with being married to him, I don't know if I have the option of not depending on him.

I brew the coffee and place my mug underneath the nozzle, filling the cup. Placing the palm of my hand on my cheek, I suck in a breath as it hurts to touch. I'm yet to look in the mirror, but I know that there will be a bruise and that my neck will probably look horrendous.

I turn the coffee machine off and carry my cup to the kitchen island, taking a seat on one of the stools and staring out of the kitchen window. It's sunny outside, a picture of perfection as I look at the gorgeous garden that stretches on for what seems like miles and miles.

This whole house is to die for, and I've never really taken time to appreciate it before. The kitchen is all marble worktops, clean white walls, grey cabinets and grey floor tiles. It's so very Nate in every way imaginable, reflecting the darkness that he harbours inside of him.

Although, I'm starting to question that darkness. I mean, there is no doubt that he is ruthless when it counts, but with me... he's different, and the more time goes on, the more I'm seeing something else inside of him... I just don't quite know what it is yet. A softness? A kindness? A desire to be more than some crime lord?

I sip my coffee, almost burning my tongue because it's too hot, when I hear footsteps behind me, and then Nate's arms are wrapping around me from behind, his chest against my back, his warmth surrounding me. I put my cup down and place my arms on top of his, and I let out a sigh.

"Good morning," he says, his voice sounding husky from just waking up.

"Morning," I say, all breathy and shit as I bask in the feel of him surrounding me.

"Have you been up long?" he enquires.

"No, just a few minutes."

I let myself sink back against him, feeling some of my tension melting away just from his touch alone. One of his arms move and comes to my face, his fingers lightly gripping my chin as he turns my head until I'm looking right at him.

His eyes roam my face, stopping on my cheek for a second before moving down to my neck. I see his jaw clench and I move my hand up and place it on his holding my chin.

"I'm fine," I say quietly with a small smile.

"That's not the point," he grates out, leaning down and placing a light kiss on my lips before moving away and to the coffee machine. I admire his ass in his grey joggers. What is it about a guy in grey joggers that gets a woman all hot and bothered? He's also not wearing a top, showing off his broad back and shoulders, all defined and hot as fuck.

He turns around and catches me staring, a smirk appearing on his face. I roll my eyes and turn away, resuming sipping my coffee now it has cooled down a little bit.

Nate joins me a few moments later, taking the seat opposite me and blocking my view of the garden. "So, we need to talk about last night," he says, his eyes looking all serious.

Oh boy.

"Okay," I reply feebly. I want to see where he goes with this, and whether he means what happened between us or what happened with the guy who cornered me.

"The guy from Purity," he begins, and I feel a little disappointment hit that he doesn't want to discuss what happened with us, but at the same time, there is a little relief too. I mean, I have no idea what last night means for our relationship, but I know something has shifted and I feel it deep inside of me.

"He was working for a woman called Jessica who used to work for me. She disappeared the day that the photos of you showed up, and I have no doubt that she is in on whatever is being planned, and she is trying to fuck with me by using you."

Oh. Wait. A woman used to work for him? The thought has me feeling something close to jealousy, and before I can stop myself, I say, "Did you fuck her?"

His eyes widen slightly at the question, and I hold his gaze.

"No." His answer has me breathing a silent sigh of relief. "Why? Does it bother you?"

"Does what bother me?"

"I don't know…. The fact that a woman worked for me? Or is it that you thought she may have been a notch on my bed post?"

"I…" I ponder his question for a moment, and I admit to myself that there is no doubt about it, I am fucking jealous… something I never thought I would be when it came to Nate Knowles. I purse my lips together, refusing to admit what he wants me to, and he chuckles quietly, sipping his coffee with a smug look on his face.

"Why would she do that?" I ask, diverting away from the previous question.

"I don't know. She had a good job here and was paid well," he admits with a shrug of his shoulders.

"Must kill you not to know something, huh?" I tease, not wanting the morning to take a nosedive when we seem to be actually having a conversation without sniping at one another.

His smile has me feeling all fucking giddy inside. Jesus.

"Anyway, today I plan to find out a bit more," he tells me.

"And how are you going to do that?" I ask, curious as to what he has planned, and kind of hoping that I can tag along because I don't want to be left here all by myself for the whole day—not after last night.

"I'm going to deal with the asshole that attacked you."

"He's not dead?"

"No, Kat, he's not dead." I breathe a sigh of relief at his words, because thinking I had possibly killed someone was freaking me out. "But he will be," he adds on, finishing his coffee and placing it down, fixing me with his stare. "And you're coming with me."

"I am?"

"Yes."

"But I don't want to see that guy ever again," I say. I don't want to be anywhere near him.

"You need to face your enemies, Kat, and this guy is your enemy as well as mine. Never shy away, never let them see your weakness. And you need to see how truly dark I can be."

"But why?" I say, my voice quiet, wondering why on earth I need to witness him doing God knows what.

"Because if you are ever to love me, you need to know every part of me." And with that, he gets up, places his cup in the sink and walks out of the kitchen, leaving me alone with the words he just said.

"Because if you are ever to love me, you need to know every part of me."

"Well, fuck."

Chapter Twenty-One

Nate

SHE LOOKS NERVOUS, but she doesn't need to be. I'm here, and it's my job to protect her—even if I was blind-sided last night by the asshole that I am about to get the truth out of.

I take her hand and lead her from the car. I can feel her hand shaking, so I pull her to my side and wrap my arm around her waist, keeping her close to me, letting her know that she has no need to be frightened.

"It's going to be okay," I tell her quietly as we enter a small house that I use for the purpose of getting rid of people. If they end up here, then their life is about to be cut short. The hidden room at my headquarters is where the torture is dragged out, but here, in this house… this is where they die.

"What if I can't handle it?" she says as we continue to walk through a hallway and enter the kitchen where there is a door that will lead us down to a basement.

"You'll be fine," I say adamantly. She's strong, she can do this. It's important that she knows me as a whole and not just the bits and pieces I let her see. I need to her witness the lengths I will go to in order to get answers. I meant it when I said to her earlier that she needed to know in order to love me.

Because I want her to love me, eventually.

She's opened my eyes to what it could be like, and I fucking want it, but I want this world I control too. It's all I know. I've lived and breathed being who I am for so long that it is a part of me, ingrained in me, and I've worked damn hard to be where I am today. The top of the chain is dangerous, there's always someone who wants to kill you, but it's the best place to be.

I open the door to the basement and lead her down the steps, keeping hold of her hand as we go. When the basement comes into view, I see two of my guys standing guard, their eyes trained on the asshole currently tied up on the floor. There are no chairs here for them to sit on, no sofa, no comforts. It's just a bare concrete floor that is cold and hard.

I stop at the bottom of the steps and indicate for Kat to stay where she is. She nods her head, her eyes a little wider than normal and she bites her bottom lip.

"Trust me," I mouth to her and again she nods her head. Good. Step one, trust, it's imperative. Crucial. Needed.

I move my fingers to my suit jacket and do the top button up. I always wear a suit because it indicates power, and it shows exactly who they're dealing with—if they didn't already know.

I walk over to the asshole tied on the floor, my shoes clicking on the concrete and echoing all around the room. When I reach him, I kick him in the back, but the sound of his yelp is muffled by the gag currently in his mouth.

"Well, well, well, what do we have here," I say tauntingly as I slowly walk around him until I am stood in front and his pitiful eyes look up at me.

"Bet you're wishing you were anywhere else but here right now, huh?" I say with a smirk on my face. Yeah, I like to play with my kills a little before I get to the deed, so sue me.

I crouch down in front of him, immediately noticing the wet patch on his trousers. "Oh dear. Had an accident, have we?" I nod to the wet patch and the guy looks like he is about to pass out. I can't be having that, not before I've got the information I need.

"Maybe this is a sign that you shouldn't fuck around with the big boys if you can't take the heat," I continue, my voice low, dangerous, deadly. "Now, I'm going to take the gag off of you, and you are going to answer some questions for me," I say, clearly indicating that he has no choice in the matter. I nod to one of my guys and they come over, bending down and removing the gag from his mouth.

He gasps and starts smacking his lips together. "Better?" I ask, although I really couldn't give a fuck.

"Water," he rasps out.

"All in good time." I pause a beat, ramping up the tension. "Now, we're going to play a game. I ask you a question, you answer, and then I will allow you one drop of water."

And I mean, one fucking drop.

I hold my hand out to the side and a bottle is quickly placed in it, along with a pipet. My guys don't need instructions, they know how I do things here.

"Tell me your name," I begin.

"Derek," he says, his voice a whisper.

I raise an eyebrow at him, waiting for the last name too.

"Hutchings. Derek Hutchings."

"Very good," I say as I open the bottle and dip the pipet in, drawing some liquid into it before holding it over the guy's mouth and squeezing out one drop. The drop misses, of course, but I don't allow him another.

"Who sent you to find my wife?" The venom in my tone increases with this question because he fucking hurt her, and I can't wait to do the same to him.

"Jessica."

Another drop of water, once again missing his mouth.

"Why?"

"To make you pay," he replies. This is easier than I thought it was going to be and thank fuck for that because I can't stand a snivelling wreck.

"Pay for what?"

"I don't know," he says, but I'm not having that.

"You mean to tell me that she sent you to find the most dangerous man's wife and you have no clue why?" If he really asked no questions, then he's thicker than he looks.

"Please," he whines, and I roll my eyes. Begging will get him nowhere with me.

"Pay. For. What?" I bite out, refusing to move on until he's answered me, or until I'm convinced he really doesn't know—which obviously I'm not buying right now.

"She... She mentioned that you had snubbed her..."

Snubbed her? What the fu... Oh hell no. This is all because I refused her ass a few months ago? Jesus fucking Christ.

"And by going after my wife she thought that I would just turn a blind eye and what? Fuck her instead?" I don't fail to notice Kat flinch out of the corner of my eye, but I keep my gaze trained on the fucker in front of me.

"I... I don't know," he replies pathetically, and at this point, I feel like I have exhausted all of his knowledge. He was simply told to do a job, probably paid poorly too, but he didn't bank on my wife being a fighter.

"You know, Derek... going after my wife was a huge fucking mistake," I say as I stand up and look down at him as he weeps on the floor. "It's not something I could ever forgive." I undo my jacket buttons and take it off, holding it out to one of my guys who quickly whips it out of my hand. I then undo my cuffs and roll the sleeves up, dominating the whole fucking room.

"Please, no," he whines as I see his panic ramp up a notch or two.

"Untie him," I instruct, and my guys walk over and cut the ropes off the bastard before they disappear behind me again. "Stand up," I tell him, and he snivels as he pathetically rolls onto his knees before pushing himself up, standing before me like the coward that he is.

"I will never entertain anyone laying their hands on what is mine, and you must know that there is no option to let you go," I say, my eyes narrowing on him.

"P… Please… Please don't," he whines, and my patience snaps. I throw my arm out, fisting my hand and hitting him right on the end of his fucking nose. His head snaps back and blood starts to spew from his nostrils, but I'm only just getting started.

I pound his body, over and over again, hitting hard, not letting up until his legs buckle from beneath him and he's led on the floor, crying, begging for his life.

I crouch over him, putting my hand around his throat and squeezing. "Does this feel good, huh?" I say to him, and he tries to shake his head but can only move ever so slightly because of my grip on him.

"No, I didn't think so. So how the fuck do you think my wife felt when you did this to her, hmm? Do you think she enjoyed it? Do you think she wanted you to squeeze the life out of her?" I say, to which his eyes almost bug out of his head.

"Answer me," I shout in his face as I let him go and his head smacks against the concrete. "Do you think she enjoyed it?" I roar, the anger flowing through me.

"No," he cries, holding his hands over his face and trying to cover himself from more potential blows.

"You left marks on her, you put your hands on her, and now I'm about to take that ability away from you," I say before I walk over to the side of the room and open a cupboard to reveal my knife collection. I pick out the butcher knife and stroll back over, bending down and grabbing his hand so quickly that he doesn't even realise what is happening until I've chopped it off, slicing the knife through his flesh. His screams echo all around us but it does nothing to stop me as I part the first hand from his body and do exactly the same to the second.

His voice becomes hoarse from the screaming as his whole body starts to shake vigorously. I couldn't give a fuck; he deserves a shitty ending. I leave the knife on the floor and stand up.

"Don't worry," I tell him as I pick up one of his hands and hold it in front of his face. "I'll make sure Jessica gets these." I intend on mailing them to her house. I know she isn't there, but someone might be, and I'll bet they let her know about the hands in the mail package that will be winging its way there tomorrow.

"Leave him to bleed out. Wouldn't want his death to be quick," I tell the guys before I turn around and finally let myself look at Kat. She's as white as a sheet, and I just hope to God that she can deal with this side of me, because if she can't then she's literally in for one hell of a ride.

"Come on," I say as I put my arm around her shoulders and move us up the steps. "Let's go home."

Chapter Twenty-Two

Kat

I HAVEN'T SAID a word since we got back to the house.

What I saw… what I witnessed… I have no idea what to do with it because my emotions are all over the damn place.

I feel weird.

On the one hand, the way he dealt with Derek was so brutal. Shocking. It went against everything I know. I've never been a violent person, and the fact that I am married to someone who can cut off someone's hands without breaking a sweat is a little frightening.

But on the other hand… he did that for me. He made it clear in that basement that I am untouchable. And the fact that he would kill for me is just… fucking mind-blowing.

I've never met someone who would want to protect me like that.

Clark was fucking useless and never defended me. I was always able to stand my own ground though, so I never saw it as an issue.

But Nate, tonight, he took it to a whole new level, and I can't deny that as shocking as it was to see, it also turned me the fuck on.

Does that make me sick?

Does it make me heartless?

Just another mindfuck to add to the list when it comes to him.

"Drink?" Nate asks as he walks past me and goes to the kitchen, and something about the way he so casually walks off snaps me out of my shock. I march down the hallway after him, entering the kitchen to see him taking a bottle of whiskey out of the cupboard.

"What the fuck was that?" I say as he pauses his movements. The silence stretches between us, and it pisses me off that he hasn't answered me. "I said, what the fuck was that, Nate?"

"That was how I deal with things," he says, still keeping his back to me.

"How you deal with things?" My voice is a little higher pitched than I would like but forgive me for being a little out of my depth here. "Jesus Christ, Nate, you cut his fucking hands off."

"And he deserved it."

"Will you fucking look at me?" I say, my frustration getting the better of me.

He turns around slowly, his eyes immediately connecting with mine and holy shit do I see a whole world of fire in his. And damn do I want to fuck him.

Does that make me messed up?

Does it mean I have less compassion than I thought I did?

"What's the matter, Kat? Can't you handle seeing me at my worst?" he asks, his tone low and deadly.

Somehow, I don't think that was him at his worst. I think there is far deeper depths to this man, and for some reason, I find myself wanting to know it all.

"I'm not going to stand here and lie to you and tell you that it didn't fucking shock me, because it absolutely did."

"Watch"—he takes one step closer to me—"Your"—and another—"Mouth." And he's right in front of me in three quick strides, making my heart race and my pussy clench.

"Why? You gonna chop my hands off if I don't?" I taunt, instantly hating myself for implying that he would hurt me.

He physically balks at my words. "Do you really think that I would hurt you?"

The look of actual hurt that crosses his face has the guilt rising up inside of me so fast that it extinguishes my worry over what happened in that basement.

"No," I answer truthfully.

"Are you scared of me, Kat?"

"Yes," I say as I feel tears start to sting the backs of my eyes. "But not in the way that you're thinking."

"Then enlighten me," he says as he puts both arms either side of my head and rests his palms on the wall behind me, caging me in.

I feel a lump rise in my throat, and I swallow it down, because this needs to be said. Just because our relationship started off in a shitty way doesn't mean that it has to be that way now. And if I am going to give myself to this man so completely, then we need to have an understanding. One where we can communicate and tell each other anything.

"I'm scared of this," I say as I move my hand up between us and place it over my heart, tapping lightly. "I hated you... like, really, truly hated you when you gave me an ultimatum. My life or marry you. I don't think I had ever despised someone so much in all my life. You took my choice away from me, something I had never had done to me before.

"But then, somewhere along the way, I realised that my life before you was merely existing, plodding along, thinking I had everything I could ever want... when actually, I had nothing. I was with a man that didn't respect me, had a business that I should have never started because Clark was a useless ass that thought of no one but himself, and I had no close friends, no relatives... it was just me, on my own.

"And then you came along. And despite the hate you made me feel, Nate, I've experienced every emotion possible since I've been with you, and more recently, those feelings of hate have started to wither, they're no longer present..." I let my voice drift off as he looks at me with something akin to hope.

"And now?" he says quietly, his breath feathering over my face.

"And now I'm scared of getting into this deeper because maybe

I'm not strong enough to survive in this world of yours. And when the time comes when I have to walk away—because we both realise that I don't fit in—I'm scared it's going to fucking break me—"

"Shut up," he says firmly, his jaw clenched.

"No, Nate, you asked me to speak so I'm fucking speaking."

"And I've heard enough of this bullshit."

"It's not bullshit, it's how I'm feeling," I say, my voice rising as anger starts to flood me. "Don't dismiss it, Nate, because I've spent my whole life ignoring the things I feel in order to make sure others are happy instead of myself."

My words hang in the air between us, silence ensuing.

"You finished?" he asks, and I nod because it seems that I have nothing left to say. I've said what I need to, I've told him my truth, so now I just have to wait for his words.

"Good. My turn," he says as he holds my stare. "Firstly, I'm not dismissing how you're feeling, Kat, but it actually fucking pains me to hear you talk about leaving, that you think you don't belong here," he says with a scoff. "Me. It pains *me*, a man who rips others apart and sends pieces to their loved ones because no fucker screws with me."

My eyes widen a little. Send pieces to their loved ones... Jesus Christ.

"I am no angel; I've done some bad shit and I will continue to be an asshole to those that do me wrong. I make no apologies for the way I do things; I own it and live with it because I've spent a lifetime in this world. I know how it works, I know the deal, and I know how to handle myself.

"But then you came along. And you know what, Kat? You scare me to fucking death."

"Me?" I say, surprised.

"Yes. You. Because as much as I am a hard bastard to everyone else, I know that you make me a better man. You make me feel too, Kat. You make me want to do right by you. My first thought every morning is you. My last thought at night is you. And every other fucking thought in-between is you.

"You don't let me walk all over you, you push me, you challenge me, and you drive me fucking insane, but I didn't realise that I needed that until you started doing it.

"I know this isn't the life you envisioned, but know this... If you ever try to leave, I will stop you. If you manage to get away, I will find you. And if you push me away, I'll push back just as hard.

"So, whatever fucked-up thoughts are going through your head right now and making you think that you don't belong by my side need to be dealt with. You do belong. You are home, Kat. Always."

My mouth feels dry, words stripped away from me. What do you say to a man that has just bared his soul to you when all he's done previously is hide himself too?

Were we always destined to find one another?

Is this where fate had been leading both of us?

To each other?

To a different happy ever after than I have envisioned?

"Nate," I whisper as I move my hands to his chest, placing them on his pecs and feeling his heart racing underneath the surface. Just like mine is. Racing, hoping, wanting it all to be true.

He moves his hand from beside me and places his over my heart too, feeling the same thump that I'm feeling beneath his skin.

"That right there," he starts, nodding his head towards my chest. "That is what makes us different. That is how we know we are meant to be. That thump, that adrenaline, that fire that we live and breathe when we're together. That's us, baby."

Oh my God.

I feel like my whole world just exploded into an array of colour. It's like I've had tunnel vision for years and now I've woken up to what is around me.

"You're mine, and I'm yours."

I'm his.

He's mine.

Fuck.

Do I let myself relish in the hope that is springing to life in my chest? The hope that I can do this, be the person he deserves, be his other half.

Do I let myself fall so completely that I wouldn't be able to breathe without him?

"But what if it all gets too much? What if I can't deal with it?" I ask, because it's a nagging thought that I know won't go away quietly.

"Then you talk to me, and we work through it together. That's what a partnership is, and you're the only person I would ever consider doing this with."

"There has never been anyone else?" I ask quietly, kind of wishing I hadn't voiced that question out loud.

"Never," he replies without missing a beat, flooring me in the process. He moves his hands and grabs both sides of my face, being careful not to push too hard on my injured cheek. "So, are we done talking? Are we clear on what is happening here?"

I look deep into his eyes and feel myself falling so fucking hard. I never thought this would happen, that this is where we would end up. I always thought I would eventually escape and live my life Nate-free. But somewhere along the way, I realised that I didn't want to do that, and staying with him has become a very real need.

"Yes."

"Good, because I'd like to fuck you before I have to go and kick some ass."

And as he carries me up to the bedroom, I feel my heart flutter, my stomach somersault, and my mind start to calm.

He wants me here.

And I need to stop being so fucking scared because he's laid it all out for me, and I need to do the same for him.

Fuck how we first met. It doesn't matter anymore. I can't keep dwelling on it and I don't want to either.

I just want to be happy, content, loved.

I think I can be that with Nate, but I guess only time will tell.

But for now, I'm going to enjoy him eating my pussy and forget about anything else.

Chapter Twenty-Three

Nate

THE BUZZING of my mobile phone wakes me, and I reluctantly roll away from Kat and look at the clock on the bedside table.

One a.m.

This can't be good.

Nothing good ever comes from my phone ringing at this hour.

With a sigh, I pick up my phone and see that a no-caller ID is showing.

I get out of the bed and take my phone with me, quickly moving to the hallway and hitting the answer button.

I wait a beat before speaking, just so I can listen to the background noise on the other end of the phone.

Breathing. Faint but it's there. I listen harder, but then a voice speaks, and I have no need to wonder about who it is anymore.

"Nate." One simple word, and enough to make my blood boil.

Motherfucking Jessica.

"I was wondering how long it would take for you to call me," I say as I move along the hallway and down the stairs to the kitchen. I have a feeling I'm going to need a bloody drink after this conversation.

"Ah, well, I didn't want to ruin the fun anytime soon, you know?" she says, and fuck if I don't want to get hold of her and wring her goddamn neck for what she has done.

"I'm a master at games, Jessica, or had you forgotten?"

"Oh, I didn't forget, Nate, I know how much you like to fuck around before you try and go in for the kill."

"There is no *try* about it. I always get my kill," I tell her, but I shouldn't need to because she already fucking knows this.

"Except this time," she taunts.

"You hope."

"I'm hidden so far away from you that you will never find me," she says.

"Is that a fact?"

"You don't think I'd come after you without a really good hiding hole, do you?"

At least she admits that she needs to hide from me. My rep is important to the role I play, and as long as she's scared then that's all that matters.

"Only cowards hide, Jessica."

"And only assholes string you along," she retorts, and I roll my eyes.

"Is this really about me not sticking my dick inside of you?" I ask her, because as reasons go, this is a truly pathetic one.

"You played me."

"I did not fucking play you. You knew where you stood with me, and you knew that it was never going to happen." I made it very clear from the off, so this is just pointless bullshit she's spouting.

"Pfft. So what about all that flirting you did, huh? All those times you said you would always take care of me, look after me, make sure I was happy…"

"That was meant in a working context only, and I told you that. I always look after my own, but I guess you took it a little too personal," I respond, not for one minute accepting this shit. "You were there when I said it to others, and I make no apologies for looking after those that look after me, but you have made the biggest mistake of your life, Jessica, because I will hunt you down, I will find you, and then I will make you wish you had never been born." I don't like the idea of hurting a woman, that's not my bag, but for this bitch, I'll make an exception.

"Because of her?" she poses it as a question, unsure of my answer.

"Yes," I say without missing a beat, because there is no fucking question, and everyone here knows it. You do not fuck with Kat. End of.

"Does her pussy taste good?" Jessica asks.

"Fucking divine." If she thought I wasn't going to answer, she was wrong.

"It's gonna hurt when I take her from you."

"And that will achieve what exactly?"

"Your misery."

Fucking hell, she's really lost the plot. How can she go from being one of my trusted people to one of my biggest problems so quickly?

"Come at me, Jessica. Give me your best shot," I say, not deterred by her threats whatsoever.

I hear a smash from upstairs and I whirl around, my heart picking up speed as it pumps wildly, and I grab a knife before my feet move to the stairs. I hear Jessica laugh and then I cut the call, the knife firmly in my grip as I move up, wanting to get to Kat quickly but knowing that I need my wits about me.

I listen, I stalk, and I move along the hallway to my bedroom. To my wife. To my motherfucking heartbeat.

The door to my bedroom is still open, and I cover all angles as I look around, the knife ready and waiting to be used in my hand.

"Shit," I hear Kat say from the ensuite, and I make my way over to the doorway, but what I see is not what I was expecting. I was expecting to have to deal with some asshole who had—somehow—managed to get in here, but what I am actually faced with is Kat sat on the edge of the sink, the bathroom mirror smashed on the floor with bits of glass everywhere.

The fucking relief I feel is ridiculous, and I start to make my way over to her.

"No, don't," she says, holding her hands up in front of her, palms facing me. "There's glass everywhere, you'll cut yourself."

It's cute that she cares, but I don't, so I continue towards her.

"Stubborn man," she mutters as I stop in front of her, managing to avoid all of the glass.

"What happened?" I ask her as I gently rest my hands on the tops of her thighs.

"I'm not sure, really. I was answering mother nature's call, washed my hands, went to wipe a smear off of the mirror and it just fucking fell." She genuinely looks puzzled, and it is just so fucking adorable.

Adorable? What the hell is wrong with me?

"Are you hurt?" I ask, my eyes running over her for any signs of cuts.

"No. I jumped up here as soon as the mirror hit the floor."

"Quick thinking," I say with a wink, and she smiles at me.

"Not just a pretty face," she says, her tone teasing.

"You are so much more than that," I say, my voice low as I move a strand of hair out of her face.

She bites her bottom lip, and it does nothing to dampen the heat that constantly burns inside of me for her.

I pull her to the edge, and she wraps her legs around me so I can carry her out of here and away from this mess.

I put her down when we get to the bedroom, and she goes to walk out.

"Where are you going?" I ask her.

"To get some shoes and a dustpan and brush."

"Get into bed," I instruct her, but she ignores me and carries on walking.

"It won't take me long, I can't leave it like that," she says over her shoulder as she disappears along the hallway.

For fuck's sake. The last thing I need is her cutting herself, I'll clean the bloody mess up. For a second, I pause. Nate Knowles. Cleaning. Being... domesticated?

Well, this is new.

I shake my head and follow her, getting to the bottom of the steps and rounding the corner to bump straight into the back of Kat. She stumbles forward, but I wrap my arm around her and pull her to me.

Why the fuck has she stopped here?

But my unspoken question is answered when my eyes drop to the floor. There, lying on the doormat—clearly having been pushed through the letterbox—are five fingers.

Immediately, I recognise the ring on one of them.

Stefan.

Fuck.

Chapter Twenty-Four

Kat

"MORE. I NEED MORE, KAT," he shouts at me, and I groan out loud.

"Can't we just take a break?" I say, exhausted from being in here for the last hour.

"Not until I'm satisfied," he says, and I fix him with my death stare. He chuckles which does nothing to dampen my annoyance. "You can look at me like that all you want, but I'm just doing my job."

"Fucking sadist," I say as I throw my fist at him, hitting the pad that he holds up in front of him.

"Good, good, harder."

I let out a cry of rage as I slam my fist again, then the other one, not even pausing when I see Nate walking up behind the man that is trying to kill me—or that's what it feels like anyway.

"How's it going?" Nate asks as he comes to the edge of the boxing ring with a smug grin on his face.

"Oh, you know, just fucking peachy," I reply as I lift my leg and kick Marlow—the trainer—in the shin.

His leg buckles and he drops to the floor.

"Now can I take a break?" I say, one eyebrow raised. Marlow just scowls at me, but I smile and walk to the edge of the ring, jumping down and grabbing the bottle of water that Nate holds out to me. Actually, I snatch the damn thing, because I'm pissed off. I've been training for the last three days and my whole fucking body hurts.

I glug down half the bottle of water and stretch my neck from side to side. I need a long fucking bath and a good book to keep me company.

"It's going well then?" Nate says as he stands there looking fucking glorious in his suit trousers and shirt, cuffs rolled up to his elbows, hands in his pockets. Christ. Even with my body and mind being mentally exhausted from everything I have learnt over the last couple of days, I'm still turned on by just his looks alone.

Damn him for being so fine.

"Nate, I know why I need to do this, but I've not stopped training for three days straight. I've been in here four times a day, not counting my session with you in the evenings. I need a fucking minute," I tell him as he looks at me with that stare that I have come to know and love. The one where he is going to act like he's punishing me for swearing, but in actual fact, he just gives me intense pleasure. Totally on board.

"Kat," he says as he steps closer and I sit on the edge of the ring, his legs moving between mine, his hands cupping my face. "I know this is hard, but you have to be prepared, and three days is nothing… If anything were to happen to you…"

"Nothing is going to happen to me," I assure him. I know he's worried, something I didn't think Nate could be, but even if something does happen, I'm not going down without a fight.

"You don't know that," he says, his jaw clenched. "Just another half an hour… for me, please?"

The fact that he is asking shocks me.

"You giving me a choice?" I say, but in a teasing manner rather than a pissed off one.

"Just this once," he says, and I laugh.

"Fine," I say with a sigh and a roll of my eyes. He swoops down and places a kiss on my lips that triggers every fucking nerve ending in my body before stepping back. I hand him my bottle of water and climb back in the ring, even as my limbs protest at the movement.

"Come on then, Marlow, let's get this done," I say as I take up the stance he's been drumming into me. One foot forward, the other back a little, my body turned slightly to one side, and hands raised in front of my face.

"You gonna kick me in the shin again?" Marlow asks, looking perplexed that I got one up on him.

"Always be aware. Isn't that your first rule?" I say to him with a smirk, and I hear Nate laugh from behind me. I see Marlow's lips twitch before he starts shouting commands at me. Left. Right. Up. Down. Do the fucking conga whilst you're at it. To be fair to Marlow, at fifty years old, he's still able to keep up, and it's all through his years of hard training and dedication.

I guess hard work really does pay off, and I have to prove that I can handle whatever is coming our way, because this isn't just about me alone or Nate on his own, this is about us, together, a team, a partnership. And there is no way that anyone is going to take my husband from me or me from him. Not now. Not ever.

"BETTER?" Nate asks me as he comes waltzing into the bathroom as I relax in the bath that I have totally overfilled with bubbles, but I don't care. I need this, and it feels so damn good.

"My muscles feel like they're in heaven," I tell him as I close my eyes and let out a contented sigh.

This bathtub is amazing with how big it is—along with the built-in seats that slope slightly so you have a gradual incline and the leather headrests around the sides for complete comfort.

When I open my eyes, I see Nate crouched by the side of the bath, his arms resting on the edge, and I can't fail to notice that he looks tired.

"Any news on Stefan yet?" I ask, but I already know the answer from the look on his face.

"No."

"You'll find him," I say, trying to reassure him.

"I just wish I knew where to start." Nate is clearly not used to not having answers by now. He's a man of great power, so to be blindsided like this must be torturing him.

When I saw those fingers on the floor after being posted through the letterbox, I was scared, worried, and feeling way out of my depth. And I know that those feelings have to be buried within me, because Nate doesn't need to be worrying about me whilst he's trying to find the man that is his best friend and his right-hand man.

"Jessica has sure done her homework," he says, and I can't help the hate I feel for a woman I have never met.

Silence ensues for a few minutes, and I try to think of any way that I can help. The thought almost makes me laugh, because not so long ago, I was looking for a way out of here, but now... now I'm getting myself in so deep and I never want to leave.

"Do you ever wish that you had a different life?" I ask quietly, and his eyes lock with mine.

"Sometimes," he admits, shocking me a little. I expected him to say no because this is who he is. Crime Lord. Ruthless. Unforgiving. But I've seen the man hiding underneath those walls of steel, and I can't help but feel a little flutter that I am the one seeing it.

"Do you ever get scared?"

"Not before you," he tells me, and fuck if I don't fall for him a little bit more. "I never had any reason to worry before you. Everyone who comes into my fold knows the deal, the risks, the very real possibility that they could die. But you... I brought you here, and I will never apologise for that because now that I have you, everything else pales in comparison... and the only thing that scares me is the thought of losing you."

Jesus.

This guy.

"Join me," I say as I gesture for him to get in. I watch as he stands up and removes his clothes, giving me an eyeful of his body that is ripped everywhere. Abs, thick thighs, muscular arms, and buns of steel. And all mine.

I move forward as he steps in so that he can sit behind me. He does and I sink back against him as his arms come around me, holding me, keeping me close.

"You know, Nate, if anyone had asked me a few weeks ago if I could be this happy with you, I'd have told them they were lying. But now, I can't imagine my life without you. I see the good in you deep down, I know that the things you do are for a reason, and while I may not like some of it, I can accept it because it's a part of you."

I turn around so that I'm facing him, straddling him with my legs.

"I've felt every emotion possible since coming here. I've hated you, despised you, wanted to run away from you and never see you again." I feel his body tense beneath me, but I'm not done yet. "But I don't feel any of those things anymore." And I take a deep breath because I am about to give him the last piece of me.

"My heart is yours, Nate. And I'm trusting you not to break it."

"Fuck," he says before planting his lips on mine and kissing me so fucking sweetly that my pussy is already wet for him. He breaks away and moves his hand to the back of my nape, holding me in place. "I love you, Kat. I'm so in fucking love with you."

My heart accelerates, and I move my hand to his dick, placing it at my opening as I slowly slide down his length. I move my hips, taking my time, relishing in the fact that this man loves me.

He actually fucking loves me.

I feel so happy right now that I could burst.

I place my lips on his, my tongue moving into his mouth as my hips slowly circle.

I swallow his groans, and he swallows mine.

And when I feel myself building, and I feel his legs tense, I move my lips away from his and tell him, "I love you, Nate."

"Fuck," he says as I keep my steady pace, not wanting this moment to be over too quickly. "Say it again."

"I love you."

"Again." He holds my stare, his hand gripping the nape of my neck, but it doesn't hurt. It feels so damn good.

"I. Love. You." And then we're both falling over the edge, our combined releases pushing us to new heights. The intensity of this moment is like nothing I could ever have imagined.

I love him.

He loves me.

And all is right with the world—for the time being, at least.

Everything else can come later.

But this is just me and him, opening the last parts of ourselves up to each other.

And as he holds me against him, his dick still inside me, I know that it's going to be a long night of repeating what we just did.

And I can't fucking wait.

Chapter Twenty-Five

Nate

"WE NEED TO FIND HIM," I tell Ronan—one of my guys.

"We're trying, boss, but we don't have a lead," Ronan says, and I sigh as I lean back in my office chair.

Why the fuck can't we find Stefan or any sign of where he may be?

I refuse to believe that he's dead. He's still out there somewhere. He has to be.

Stefan and I have been in this together for years. Since school. Our friendship goes back decades. He's always been by my side.

I rub my temples as I try to rid myself of the dull ache that has been getting progressively worse since this morning.

I've been scouring my computer since I got up. I've had my guys go over to Stefan's apartment yet again, just to check to see if they missed anything. They didn't. And I've been there myself, so I know there's nothing. It's just false hope right now.

"I don't mean to interrupt, but I thought you guys might like some coffee," Kat says as she carries a tray with two mugs into my office. I smile at her as she comes to my desk, stopping and placing the tray down. She's put a jug of milk on the tray, along with a sugar bowl and some biscuits. Cute.

"Thank you," I say, and she gives me a small smile.

"Found anything yet?" she asks, and I hate that I have to admit that I haven't.

"No."

I gesture for Ronan to take his mug and he thanks Kat before adding milk and sugar.

"Yours is made how you like it. I only brought the milk and sugar for him," she says with a wink and a tip of her head in Ronan's direction. Is this what domesticated looks like? If so, I'm fucking happy with it.

"Can I help?" she says, and I don't miss the fact that she looks a little nervous about asking that question.

"You can actually," I reply, and she instantly relaxes. "You can get ready because we're going out."

"We are?"

"Yes. Dress in something comfortable."

She leaves my office to go and get ready, but I could bet my life on it that she isn't expecting me to take her to a gun range. She needs to learn to shoot. And quick.

AS SHE STANDS there in tight jeans, a loose tee which hangs down one of her shoulders to reveal her lightly tanned skin beneath, hair hanging down her back in loose waves, ankle boots, goggles on her face and a gun in her hand, I don't think I've ever seen anything so sexy before in my life.

She's concentrating, her eyes trained on the target as she gets ready to pull the trigger. And when she fires and makes the hit straight in the heart, I feel my dick twitch.

Fucking hell. I should have brought her here sooner because this is an image that I never knew I needed.

We've been here for the last hour, and so far, her gun training is going better than I expected. Having never picked up a gun before, she's a natural, and it is just another confirmation that she belongs with me.

She fires a few more shots, hitting the mark every time. She's got a good eye for this, and I have to say that I am more than a little relieved because I don't want her to be a sitting duck.

A woman that can handle herself and handle me... never thought I'd ever find her, but I did, and although I'm actually fucking scared that she could be taken from me, I'm also liking that I have someone to protect so fiercely that I would do anything for them. Of course I've always taken care of my people, but for her, it's just so much more.

She turns around, dropping her hands and holding the gun at her side as she looks at me.

"How did I do?" she says with a smug smile.

"You did good."

"Just good?" she says as her eyes narrow on me slightly.

"Well, it could just be beginners' luck," I tease.

"Pfft. I did great, and you know it."

"Never had any doubt," I say as I stand up and walk over to her, wrapping my arms around her and placing a kiss on the top of her head. But our moment of quiet and happiness is short-lived as a loud explosion sounds from somewhere outside the building.

"What the fuck was that?" she says, and I have no time to tell her about her mouth because the sound of gunshots rings loud in my ears.

I quickly grab her hand and pull her down the walkway at the side of the range, practically dragging her as I aim to get us to the other end and hidden behind the Perspex and targets, giving us some sort of shield at least.

I hear commotion coming from just outside the room and I duck down, pulling her with me until we are concealed by the half-wall partition.

"Baby, I realise you've only just had your first gun lesson but fill the fucker up and get ready to use it," I whisper as I pull some bullets out of my pocket and hand them to her. She was shown how to load the gun before she started firing, and she quickly springs into action. I do the same with the gun I pull from the waistband of my jeans at the back, and I get ready to shoot any fucker that comes within my line of sight.

"Jesus," she says as she finishes loading the gun and clicks off the safety, having it ready in her hands and trained in front of her as she crouches on the floor, pointing it up the walkway we just came down.

Voices can be heard just outside, and I put my finger to my lips, indicating for her to be quiet as I tap into my senses and keep my ears alert.

Footsteps sound heavy on the hardwood floor as they enter the room, and if my skills are anything to go by, then I count four sets of feet in this room. Fuck. We're outnumbered, but I know that Kat and I will fight to the fucking death, so bring it on assholes.

The footsteps come to a halt, and it is like time stops.

"They were here," a voice says, and I immediately recognise it as Alessandro—Jessica's brother. Of course this is to do with Jessica, that psycho bitch isn't going to give up anytime soon. I can only hope that she is here somewhere so I can end this shit once and for all.

"They're hiding somewhere," another voice says, but this one I don't recognise.

"No shit," Alessandro says sarcastically. "Split up." And then it goes quiet except for the sounds of feet moving around the room. We're fucking cornered, and there is no way out. If they find us here, then we're likely to have a serious problem, so the only thing to do is face them head on and take them out.

I allow myself a brief look at Kat, and I expect to see her hands shaking, but they're not. She has concentration written all over her face, and her finger is on the trigger of her gun. I place my lips by her ear and whisper as quietly as I can. "We need to take them out, so on three, we're going to slowly move up and shoot them until they're all dead."

I hear her breathing deepen, but I don't give her time to think as I count down.

"One... Two... Three..."

I move to the half-wall and she does the same, and pushing myself up slowly, I peer over, seeing two of the fuckers prowling along where we were stood minutes ago.

I train my gun on one of them, and Kat takes my lead, training her gun on the other.

"Pull the trigger in three… two… one…" I whisper, and then the sound of our guns firing echoes around the room. I hit my mark, the bullet lodging straight in the guy's head. He drops to the floor like a sack of shit, and I see Kat's mark double over. She hit him in the stomach, but I take no chances and I fire a bullet into the top of his head as he's bent over.

Two down.

"You did great, baby," I tell her as I look for any other signs of life. A movement to the left of the room catches my eye, and I don't hesitate as I aim and shoot. It hits and they grunt before disappearing. Just because I can't see them doesn't mean they are dead yet, so we still need to be wary.

"Wow," I hear Kat say on a breath. "Never thought I'd get turned on by seeing you with a gun, but damn…"

I chuckle quietly. "Time for that later. Right now, we gotta kill the last fucker in this room and make sure the one I just took out is actually dead."

She nods and my eyes keep moving around the room, but there is no sign of anyone else. Maybe there were only three after all?

But no sooner have I thought the words than a bullet comes whizzing past me, missing me by fucking millimetres. Kat gasps and I duck her down, needing her out of the firing line. Another bullet fires as I duck down next to her, and I have to wonder who the fuck taught the other person to shoot, because their aim is shit.

I crawl along the floor on my stomach, needing to get out of this goddamn corner. The shots keep coming, but they're all trained on the direction I just came from. Good, they clearly have a shit aim and the crappy sense to not realise that I can move along this walkway instead of sitting on my ass in the corner and waiting it out. I quickly look behind me, seeing Kat mimicking my movements, and I thank fuck that she has the common sense to not cry like a girl and freak the hell out. She's fierce and strong, and I know that she will have my back at every turn. I reach the end and peer round, seeing nothing but the guys we already took out lying on the floor. I slowly move my way along, almost sliding on the wooden flooring. We stay out of sight until we come to the other walkway that goes down the other side of the room. This is it. Do or die time.

I hear feet moving towards me, and from my position on the floor, I take full advantage of being low to the ground and waiting for this fucker to come into view. Feet appear in my vision seconds later, and my gun fires, shooting the bastard in the shin. A cry of pain rings out, and I move my gun and eyes higher, hitting the kneecap. And higher, hitting the chest. And when I look up and meet Alessandro's eyes, I smirk before raising the gun higher and hitting him right between the eyes.

I quickly move to my feet and check that the other guy I took out is dead, which he is. I don't think too much as I lean down and grab Kat's hand, pulling her to her feet and making sure we get the hell out of here before any other shit can go down.

Bodies line the halls as we move, and I step over them as if this is just another day at the office—which it totally is for me.

I stop at every turn and do a quick scan of our surroundings before leading us to the front doors and seeing my men stood there, waiting, watching, guns in hand.

I open the doors and Mitchell—a guy who has worked for me for the last five years—looks at us and I see him physically breathe a sigh of relief. He nods to the car, and I know that these guys will make sure that we are covered. I have no reason to doubt that they have already taken out anyone else that just tried to ambush us.

I quickly open the car door and push Kat in the back, me following behind her before the door is closing and one of my guys drives us the fuck out of here.

Chapter Twenty-Six

Kat

JESUS. Go to a gun range and—ironically—get gunned down. Not quite how I thought our outing would end up.

Nate was amazing as he sprang into action, and I'm so glad I was able to help somewhat—even if he did have to cover my ass because my aim was off. I'm not going to dwell on it though. I mean, it was my first damn lesson, and I found myself in one hell of a life-or-death situation.

Nate has been holed up in his office since we got back, some of his men in there with him whilst I've taken a shower and made some food. I'm not really hungry, so the lasagne I made is sat warming in the oven.

I could have lost him today, and I know that it would have broken me. I have no doubt that if anything had happened to me then it would have broken him too. We are so in fucking sync with one another that it scares me, but I want to embrace it and revel in the fact that we are on the same wavelength.

I sigh as I roll my shoulders, feeling the tension that resides there. I have so much pent-up energy and I need to expel it. I decide to go and work it out in the boxing room at the bottom of the garden. I go to my bedroom and get changed—although, I no longer sleep in here because I'm always in Nate's bed now, so this is just a room where I keep my clothes.

I put on my mid-thigh cycle shorts and a crop top before tying my hair up in a high ponytail. I wipe the makeup from my face and look at myself in the mirror.

I have a glow about me. My cheeks are slightly flushed, and my eyes have a fire inside of them that was lacking before I met Nate. It's almost nice to have a purpose in life—even if it is as part of the crime world where you could take your last breath at any moment.

I put on my trainers and make my way back down the stairs and out of the patio doors at the back of the house. I don't bother Nate with where I'm going because he's busy and my whereabouts isn't important right now. I'm here, I'm not leaving the grounds, so I have no reason to bother him.

I walk briskly and enter the code on the panel by the door when I reach it, opening the door and stepping inside before entering the code again to lock myself in. Nate is the only other one that can get in here, so I needn't be worried about any of his men walking in.

Turning on the sound system, I type in Linkin' Park and hit play, turning the volume up and letting it vibrate through the walls and floor.

I tape up my hands, preferring to do that rather than wear gloves. I've found that I like to feel the hit on my skin with no gloves to act as a buffer. I don't know, it soothes me, I guess.

I move to the mat and do a quick warm-up, stretching and getting my body ready. Today was meant to be my day of rest from this, but I know it will help me, and even though my body is tired, I get such a rush from doing this.

I finish stretching and move to the bags, picking one and starting to hit it with a steady rhythm. There are five bags in a row—with space between each one—and I have to wonder why there are five in the first place. I know that none of Nate's men work out in here, so there's no need for so many, but it's not my place to question it.

I time my hits to the beat of the music, losing myself and trying to empty my mind of anything other than feeling the burn.

I hit, I kick, I work my whole body, my breathing deepening, my skin feeling like it's on fire. I work through five songs, each one fuelling me to do better, be faster, hit harder. I feel the sweat coating my body, but it still doesn't feel like enough. I'm still thinking too much. I need my thoughts to come to a halt because there are too many questions I can't answer right now.

What is the deal with this Jessica chick?

Why is she coming after Nate so hard?

Is it really just because he knocked her back?

Is there more to the story?

What the hell would have happened if he had died today?

What would I have done?

How would I have coped without him?

How have I managed to come to rely on him so quickly over the last few weeks?

I let out a cry of rage as I move my arms quicker, feeling the pain in my knuckles but not caring. I know the skin has broken despite the wraps around my hands. I can feel the fabric chaffing on my skin, but I refuse to stop.

I keep going, struggling for breath until I feel arms wrap around the back of me, stopping me from moving as they lock tight, my arms pinned by my sides.

I know it's Nate from the feel of him. I didn't hear him come in, but then I wouldn't because the music is loud, and I was totally focussed on hitting the fucking bag.

He doesn't say anything as he pulls me away from the bag and moves me to the boxing ring, turning me around and sitting me on the edge. I breathe deeply, trying to get oxygen into my lungs.

There's a towel in his hand, and he brings it to my face, wiping my skin gently before moving it down my neck and to my stomach. He wipes away the evidence of my workout, running the towel along every part of my exposed flesh. And when he's done, he lifts my arms up before removing my crop top, allowing him to wipe my breasts.

My eyes meet his, mesmerised by his actions, but his are trained on my body, on what he is doing. My breath falters as his fingers move to the top of my shorts and I lift my bum slightly, letting him slide them down my legs—along with my knickers—until he removes them completely, as well as my shoes and socks. He runs the towel over me as he crouches between my legs, his eyes finally connecting with mine when he gets to my pussy.

My heart pumps wildly, but it's no longer because of the work-out. It's for him. All for him.

And when he pushes my legs apart, stretching me as much as he can, I feel the heat rise inside of me. I'm exposed for him, completely at his mercy, and so fucking turned on.

He holds my stare for a beat before he breaks it and buries his face in my wetness. Yeah, I'm already wet for him, and I will make no apologies for that. I've never gotten wet just from looking at a guy before, but for him, my body just responds without me telling it to.

He licks up and down before burying his tongue inside of me. I drop my head back, my eyes rolling when his finger replaces his tongue and then his mouth is back on my clit.

I move my hand to my breast, pinching my nipple, feeling his free hand come over mine, urging me to pinch harder.

I groan out loud, and he adds another finger to the one already moving in and out of me. He stretches me, sucking my clit, setting every nerve-ending alight.

"Fuck," I shout as he moves his tongue in circles, and I drop back against the ropes that go around the perimeter of the ring, my one arm no longer able to support me.

I feel my body start to tremble as I barrel towards my release. Dear God, what this man can do with his mouth is a pure gift.

And just when he is working me into a frenzy, he removes his mouth and fingers, quickly replacing them with his cock. He drives into me, and I scream out, my fingers looking for something to hold onto and finding the ropes that I lean against. I grip on tightly as he hits my core, sending me higher and higher. And when he brings his thumb to my clit and his mouth to my nipple, I fall so fucking hard.

My walls clench around him as I call out his name.

My body shakes as he swallows my cries with his mouth, his fingers returning to my nipple and pinching deliciously.

I hungrily devour him, needing more. I always need more. I'm becoming so fucking needy for him it's ridiculous.

I squeeze his cock harder, my walls clamping around him, and he roars into my mouth, but I don't let him break away as I move my arms around his neck and hold him tight. I take great fucking pleasure in making him come hard. It's a beautiful thing.

The music still plays around us as we pant and try to regain our breath—and the use of my limbs for me.

I move my lips to his ear and feel so overcome with emotion. "I love you," I whisper, and he holds me closer, his cock still inside of me.

I never want us to lose this feeling.

The want, the desire, the lust.

And I also never want us to lose the love that is between us.

The power, the ferocity, the feral way in which we need each other.

It's our type of love. It's stunning, delicious, and dangerous.

And I wouldn't have it any other way.

Loving a dangerous man has more perks than cons, even if it did take me a while to see it.

Chapter Twenty-Seven

Nate

"ZOEY," I say when I open the door as she storms in with a face like thunder.

"What the hell, Nate?"

Oh dear, she's pissed. I close the door and stifle a groan before I turn around to face her.

"Why is there double the amount of security at Purity? And why are there now four guys watching me twenty-four-seven instead of just the bog-standard two?" she questions, and I run my hand through my hair, taking a breath.

"And why haven't you picked up the phone to me the last couple of days? And how the hell is Kat? I haven't spoken to you since what happened at Purity with her, and I swear to God, Nate, you are walking a fine line with me."

Dear God, it's too early for this shit.

I walk past her and into the kitchen, needing more caffeine. I see Kat sat at the kitchen island, and I go to her and place a kiss on her lips before turning to the coffee machine.

"Honestly, Nate, you can't just keep me out of the goddamn

loop all the time," Zoey continues as she enters the kitchen and sees Kat sat there. "Oh, hey, Kat," she says, all cheery as she goes to the island and takes a seat beside my wife. Her whole demeanour has changed in a split second, and I'm quite glad Kat is here as a buffer. When my sister is on one, well, it usually just ends with me copping a load of earache—even if what I am doing is in her best interests.

They both start chatting, both of them animated and clearly happy to see one another.

I make the drinks and refill Kat's cup before joining them, sitting opposite.

"So?" Zoey says as she stops talking to Kat and pins me with her stare. "What's going on, Nate?"

I glance at Kat, and she smiles behind her coffee cup. I think she enjoys seeing Zoey give me shit. The only other woman that can get away with doing so.

"Things have gotten worse with Jessica," I begin, and then I fill her in on Stefan, and what happened at the gun range yesterday.

When I've finished, Zoey just looks at me, no reaction at all.

"I'm sorry I haven't come to see you, but it's been a clusterfuck of a few days," I admit.

"There is such a thing as a phone, Nate," Zoey says, and I can't argue with her because she's right. I should have just called her, but my mind has been elsewhere... namely on my beautiful wife and her pussy.

"I know... I'm sorry," I say, because that is all I can say. I want to keep the two women that I love safe, and I'll apologise for not telling her sooner, but I won't apologise for upping security measures.

"Do you still have no idea where Jessica is?" Zoey asks, and I painfully shake my head to admit that I don't.

"Jesus, how can she have slipped the net like this?" Zoey questions out loud, and it's the very thing I keep asking myself.

"You know, there is one way that might work for getting her to crawl out of her hole..." Kat says, her voice fading off as she bites her bottom lip and sets her cup down.

Zoey and I both look at her and I nod for her to continue.

"I mean, she wants me, right? So, why not put me in contact with her? I could—"

"Absolutely fucking not," I interrupt, enraged that she would think I would put her in harm's way like that.

"Nate, just listen—"

"No, not happening." I cut her off again, not needing to hear anymore.

"For fuck's sake, will you listen to me?" Kat says, exasperated already, and I narrow my eyes on her.

"She wants you dead," I say deadpan. "She wants to get to me through you. In what universe would I ever entertain the idea of you going near her?"

"Because it's the only thing you have left," Kat says adamantly, and the silence stretches between the three of us for a beat. "You have no idea where Stefan is, or if he is even alive, and your resources are not working."

I grind my teeth together, hating that she is voicing what I already know.

"I'm not saying I'll go in blind… she just has to think I am," Kat continues. "I'm not totally useless, and I am partly to blame for all of this."

My face morphs into shock. "How the fuck are you in any way to blame for this?"

"If I wasn't here, this wouldn't be happening, and you damn well know it."

"Not true."

"Of course it is. She hates that I'm married to you. She wants you, and for some reason, she thinks taking me out of the equation is going to make that happen."

"And what exactly are you suggesting here, Kat?" I ask, because nothing about this idea is watertight.

"I'll make contact with her and arrange a meet up… and then play it by ear from there," she says with a shrug. Yes, a goddamn shrug. My mouth actually falls open, and Zoey laughs. Do these women think this is all a big joke?

"I can help too," Zoey says, encouraging this ridiculous idea.

"No," I say again, because they clearly didn't hear me the first two times.

"Come on, Nate," Kat urges. "You need to end this."

"I am fully aware, but I am not sending my wife and my sister into the fucking firing line," I rage as I stand up and pace the floor. "I'm going to make some calls, and when I get back, I hope that all common sense has returned because you've obviously both lost your minds."

With that, I leave the kitchen and make my way to my office.

Fucking hell, as I if I would ever let them go through with such a stupid idea, not to mention one of the shittiest plans I've ever heard.

Everything about that suggestion has disaster written all over it, and over my dead body will I ever let happen.

Chapter Twenty-Eight

Kat

"HE'S GOING to fucking kill us," I say to Zoey, but all she does is give me a cheeky grin.

"You can handle him," she says. "And I've had years of practice, so it'll be fine."

I don't agree with her, but we're here now, so it's time to see it through.

We walk into the strip club, the smoky atmosphere hitting me as soon as we enter—along with the musty smell and scent of alcohol. I stop myself from screwing my face up and remind myself that I have my big girl pants on. I can do this. We can do this. And everything will be fine.

Yeah, play it on a loop, Kat, because Nate may very well kill you himself after this.

I don't know this Jessica chick, but the fact that she worked here before working for Nate surprises me. Zoey told me that Nate hired her after seeing some guy beating on her outside of this place one night. I didn't ask what Nate was doing here and it was way before I even knew he existed, so it is of no concern to me. It does make me wonder what the hell she's doing though, turning her back on someone who saved her.

"Yo, Jerry," Zoey shouts from beside me, making me startle.

I look in the direction of this Jerry guy to see a man with almost no hair, a cigarette hanging out of his mouth, stubble that needs a good shave, and a vest with holes in that does nothing to cover the beer belly that he is sporting. Lovely.

"Well, well, if it ain't Zoey Knowles," Jerry says, his voice raspy. Probably from the fifty-a-day cigarettes he smokes, no doubt.

"No need for pleasantries, Jerry, you know I don't come here unless I want something," Zoey continues, moving to the bar but not touching it. Jerry turns slightly on his stool, and I can literally hear the wood creak from the movement.

"Who's your friend?" he asks, a smirk on his face and a lecherous look in his eyes. Gross.

"Nate's wife, so don't even think about it," she warns, and he rolls his eyes before taking a puff of his cigarette and flicking the ash on the floor.

"What do you want?" he says, and I'm relieved we are about to cut through the bullshit.

"I need to know if you have seen or heard anything from Jessica," Zoey asks, and Jerry looks at his cigarette thoughtfully.

"And what's it worth to me?" he says.

"Five grand," Zoey answers. She'd already told me that this was how it would go down, so I'm not shocked.

"Five grand, huh?" he says as he twirls the cigarette in his fingers before putting it back in his mouth. "And what might you want with her?"

"None of your business," Zoey retorts.

"Oh, it is my business if I tell you," he replies with a shit eating grin on his face, cigarette stuck in the corner of his mouth.

"Do you want the five K or not?" I say, not waiting for Zoey to answer him.

He looks at me, his eyes roaming up and down my body, but I just lift my chin a bit higher. He's not going to intimidate me. I live with Nate, for fuck's sake, and if he doesn't scare me then this asshole won't either.

"She came here a few weeks ago, looking for Percy, said she needed a word," Jerry says as he holds his hand out for the money. Zoey slaps a wad of notes in his hand and his eyes light up. "She left with Percy that day and I haven't seen her since."

"Hmmm. Really?" Zoey questions, and I know she doesn't believe that he knows nothing else.

He nods and takes one last puff before stubbing his cigarette out in the ashtray. At least he didn't use the floor this time.

"I haven't seen Percy since either," Jerry confirms, as if this concludes business.

"May I?" Zoey says as she points to his cigarette packet on the bar counter.

"Taken up the habit again, huh?" he replies as he gestures for her to take one. She leans across and scoops up the packet, removing one and popping it between her lips. I stare at her, puzzled. What the hell is she doing?

"One won't hurt. Got a light?" she asks, and Jerry reaches into his pocket and places the lighter in her hand.

"Thanks." She lights it up and hands him back the lighter, taking a puff and blowing the smoke out in front of her.

"Tastes good, huh?" Jerry asks, and Zoey smiles.

"You have no idea," she says before she quickly moves and stubs the cigarette out on the back of his hand which is resting on the bar.

He squeals and clenches his teeth as his skin burns.

"Tell me where the fuck she is," Zoey says, her teeth bared in his face as I stand here like a spare part. I see Jerry move his other hand, and I act before thinking, taking the gun out of the back of my jeans and placing it at the back of his head.

"I wouldn't," I warn him, and he drops his hand, letting it dangle beside him.

"You been training her up," he comments, and Zoey smirks.

"Nah. She was one of us way before she came into the fold." Her answer makes my chest feel like its swelling with pride. Funny, at the start of all this it would have made me feel sick, but not now.

Now I own that fact that my husband is a badass, and that my sister-in-law is like a chip off the old block.

"Now, do you really want to tell us where she is?" Zoey says, and I nudge the gun, just reiterating the fact that I could blow his brains out any second now. I find it strange that not one person has batted an eyelid at this exchange, and the women keep dancing, prancing around on stage with their boobs on show and only a piece of fabric covering their modesty. Although, I'm sure that comes off too at some point. It's not exactly a respectable place.

"Fuck," he spits, sweat beading on his brow.

"Well?" she pushes and removes the cigarette from his hand, revealing a very nasty burn mark.

"She's at The Lodge," he says.

"With?" Zoey continues.

"Percy and three others."

"Who?"

"Brock, and then two I don't know."

"If you're fucking lying to me, I'll be back, and I'll make sure my brother comes too," she threatens, and I swear to God that Jerry is about to piss his pants.

"We're done here," Zoey says, and I lower the gun to my side but keep my finger on the trigger, just in case. I may have only had one lesson, but I know how to shoot if needed.

And then we walk out of the strip club as if nothing has happened and back to the car.

"Well, that was worth it," I say as I buckle up and Zoey sits in the driver's seat and starts the car.

"I'm surprised that Nate didn't get the info that we just did," she ponders as she pulls us out of the car park.

"Maybe he didn't check here?" I hedge.

"Oh, he definitely checked here, but I'm betting that every time he's come around, Jerry has been conveniently busy—as in, he's scarpered and hidden until the coast has cleared."

"So why didn't he scarper from you?" I ask, because she can hold her own as much as Nate can.

"Because I'm not the one that has a thirst for blood, so I'm the easier one to deal with out of the two of us. And I don't usually get involved in this side of things, so they don't expect it, but I've had to recently…" Her voice drifts off and she clamps her mouth shut like she's said too much.

"What do you mean?" I ask, because I am not letting this go. There is clearly a story here.

"Nothing."

"Come on, Zoey, don't try and bullshit me. I thought we were friends?"

"Oh, you did not just chuck that in my face," she says with shock on her face. "I've not had a friend in so fucking long, so don't you dare—"

"Best not keep secrets then," I interrupt, and she eyes me, her eyes not focussing on the road, but I hold her stare. To survive in this family, you have to be strong, and I'm learning just how strong I am with every day that passes.

"Damn you, Kat Knowles," she says, and I laugh as she looks back to the road with a smile on her face. "I knew I liked you from the first moment I met you."

"Yeah, yeah, I fit like a glove, yada, yada… now, spill."

"Promise me that you won't tell Nate," she says, and I groan out loud.

"Don't make me do that. Don't make me lie to my husband."

She's silent a beat before she stops the car at a red set of lights and looks to me. "You really love him, don't you?"

"Yes." I don't hesitate, because there is no reason to. I do love him. So fucking much.

She gives me a soft smile. "I'm so happy you found each other."

"Me too," I say as I feel emotional all of a sudden. I don't think she knows how we met, and I don't plan to tell her. It's our business, and we've come so far since that day.

My phone starts to ring in my pocket, and I already know it will be Nate without even looking at it.

"Better answer that and get it over with," Zoey says as she starts driving again, the lights now green—although they could have been green for a while, and I would have no idea because we were talking.

"Hi, babe," I say, a bit too cheerily, as I answer the phone.

"Where are you?" he asks, and I can hear the edge to his voice.

"Just with Zoey."

"Doing what?"

"Driving."

"Uh huh. And why did you feel the need to sneak out of here and not tell me?" he says, and I desperately try to search for a way to tell him where we're going without him getting all stressed out.

"You were busy." I roll my eyes at myself and my short answers.

"I'm never too busy for you," he says, and damn if my heart doesn't melt a little bit at the way he says it.

"I know, but I just thought it was better to let you calm down and not bother you."

"Bullshit, Kat. Now tell me where you are."

Damn him. I'm going to have to tell him.

"We're just—" I'm cut off from saying anything else as my phone is swiped from my hand. "Hey!" I say to Zoey as she puts the phone by her ear.

"Big bro, don't worry, we won't be gone long," she says sweetly, and I can imagine Nate is about ready to blow a fuse. "We'll call when we're on the way back."

"ZOEY, DON'T YOU DARE—"

"Oops," she says as she cuts the call and pockets my phone.

"He's going to be so pissed at you," I tell her with a grin.

She shrugs her shoulders. "It's nothing I haven't dealt with before."

I can't help but laugh as I hear my phone ringing again. And again. And again.

"We'll be back there soon anyway, and then he'll be able to shout at us," I say, because he will probably do lots of shouting.

"Uh huh," she says as she continues to drive, but when she misses the turning to take us back, I furrow my eyebrows.

"Where are we going?"

"To The Lodge."

"Zoey, no," I say. "Don't be stupid, we can't go there."

"We can, and we are," she replies adamantly.

"We got the information we needed, now let's just get back and tell Nate what we know."

"No."

"No?" Jesus Christ, she's gone all Thelma and Louise on my ass. "Zoey, we're not prepared for anything like this."

"Speak for yourself. I've got ammo and guns galore in the trunk, a few grenades and some knives. Oh, and there's a knuckle duster if you're feeling like you want to be hands-on."

I'm momentarily stunned. This can't be happening. We're not doing this.

"Pull over," I tell her, but she ignores me. "Pull the damn car over, Zoey," I say, and she comes to an abrupt halt at the side of the road, almost launching me into the bloody windscreen.

I unbuckle and open the door, jumping out of the car and taking a few deep breaths.

Jesus Christ, she can't be serious. I can't do this. I'm a shitty option for a sidekick. I've only ever fought beside Nate, and even then, he covered my ass.

Oh dear lord, this is not how it was supposed to go.

"Kat, look at me," Zoey says as I hear her voice behind me.

I turn around and pin her with my stare, and all I see is that steely determination that comes from being a Knowles.

"You can do this. I need you to do this with me."

"Why? Why can't we leave this to Nate and help him that way?" I say, desperately hoping I can reason with her.

"And if we do that then he'll charge in there and it will be the first time he will have ever laid his hands on a woman in that way because he's past the point of patience with that bitch, and then all hell will break loose. He would never forgive himself for killing a female. It goes against everything he stands for."

"He might not," I argue back pathetically, and she quirks one eyebrow at me. "Yeah, okay, he would probably do that, but he'd take a shitload of back up with him."

"Yes, he would, but I've got back up ready and waiting, so we don't need to worry about that," she says, flooring me again.

"Who? How? When?"

She chuckles. "Don't worry about that. Just know that there are some badass MC's that owe me a favour or three, so I called it in, and they'll meet us a few miles back from The Lodge."

Well. Fuck.

"Now are you in?" she asks.

Am I in?

Am I going to deceive my husband by not telling him? I mean, technically, I can't because Zoey has my phone, but still… it doesn't feel right.

"I don't like him not knowing," I tell her, and her eyes soften despite what we are about to do.

"Is that a yes?"

I sigh. "It's a yes."

"I knew you wouldn't let me down," she says with a smile, and I try to return it, but I feel shitty. "You and me, we're gonna be best mates, Kat, I just know it."

I have to laugh, because honestly, I can see it too, no matter how crazy she may be at times.

"Now, come on," she says as she goes back to the driver's side of the car and gets in. I sink into the passenger seat and shut the door, and then we're off, speeding away and towards what could be the biggest mistake of our lives.

"We've got this," she says, and I turn my head to look at her. She's determined, and she would do anything for Nate, same as I would.

We're doing this to blindside Jessica, and to save Nate from himself.

"We've got this," I say, and Zoey smiles. "Now, you best tell me what you were going to say earlier, before we got interrupted."

"Damn, I was hoping you would have forgotten about that," she says, and I laugh.

"Ha ha, you wish. Now spill."

Chapter Twenty-Nine

Nate

FUCKING HELL, I'm about to blow a gasket.

I've been ringing Kat and Zoey's phones non-stop for the last fifteen minutes, and neither of them have answered. I knew I shouldn't have left them alone together. Fucking dangerous.

"Find them," I bark to the four men in my office. They quickly move and leave, knowing that I am so close to losing my shit.

I knew I should have fitted Zoey's car with a fucking tracker. Damn me for trying to have some sort of morals.

I run my hands through my hair and grip as the phone call once again goes to voicemail.

I march from my office and down the stairs, grabbing my car keys from the hook by the door and I make my way outside and to my car. I can't just sit here, I need to drive, keep my eyes peeled for any goddamn sign of my sister and my wife.

I get in the car and am about to start it when my phone buzzes in my hand.

.   .   .

ZOEY: The Lodge.

THE LODGE? Why the fuck would she be there? It's over in the next town, and there is no reason for them to be going on a goddamn jolly right now.

I quickly dial Kurt's number and wait for him to pick up. Three rings later, I'm about to blow, when he answers.

"Kurt," I bark sharply. "I need some intel on who the hell is staying at The Lodge."

He doesn't speak, but I hear him tapping keys on a keyboard, and I presume he's looking at security cameras and finding the right one.

"It looks empty," he says a few moments later as I put him on loudspeaker and place the phone in the car holder. I reverse on the drive and tear down the driveway and to the main road.

"There has to be someone there," I say, refusing to believe that Zoey and Kat would be going to an abandoned place.

"Seriously, there's no cars and no movement..." His voice trails off and I sigh as I realise that I'm clearly going to have to wait for answers until I get there.

"Wait a minute," he says as I hear a few more keys tapping, and I run through a set of red lights because fuck that shit. I'm not waiting for nothing or nobody.

"Shit," I hear him say down the phone before he sucks in a breath.

"What is it?" I say urgently.

"Jessica."

"Pardon?"

"It's Jessica. She's there."

Oh my God. No. No, no, no. They wouldn't...

"Alert everyone and have the house guarded and the rest of the men coming after me as back up."

The line goes dead, and I curse to the high heavens. I push my foot down on the accelerator, needing to be there fifteen fucking minutes ago.

If anything happens to either of them, I am going on a fucking killing spree.

And if they happen to make it out with a hair on their heads out of place, let's just say that whoever is responsible won't like the rage that I will unleash upon them.

Kat

"I have a bad feeling about this, Zoey," I say as we make our way on foot up to this Lodge place.

"Relax," she says as if we're just going for a quiet evening stroll. "These guys will have our backs." She points to what I can only describe as the Motley crew behind us. There are six of them, and they all look pretty mean, and I don't trust any of them. I'm starting to doubt my trust in Zoey at this point. I should have fought harder to get my phone off of her, but I know why she is doing this.

Nate won't get over killing a woman. She told me that, and I believe it. He may be ruthless, but he only kills men.

I almost laugh at the thought. I mean, killing men is bad enough, but I don't know, there's just something about him not laying a hand on a female that makes my heart beat a little harder for him.

"Besides, Nate will be here soon," she says, and I stop walking, my mouth dropping open.

"What?" I almost screech.

"I text him about five minutes ago, so we have about fifteen left before he starts to get anywhere close."

"Zoey, you can't just keep springing shit on me and expecting me to be able to deal with it," I tell her, exasperated.

"Welcome to the family, babes," she says, a smile on her face.

It's so hard not to give into her when she's being like that, because it's hard to stay mad at her, but so God help me, she is putting us at so much risk here.

"I think we should wait for Nate," I say, even though we were doing it for him.

"Fine," she says with a shrug of her shoulders before she turns her back on me and continues walking.

"What the hell are you doing?" I say as I jog to catch up with her.

"I'll go alone."

"Zoey, stop it, I'm not letting you go alone," I tell her with a sigh as I fall into step beside her. Nate would kill me for letting her do this without any help. I don't trust these biker guys, and I don't think Zoey should be relying on them either.

"We're nearly there and then we can get this over with and go back home and crack open a bottle of wine," she declares, and I huff at her.

"If you say so."

"I do." She nods. "We've got weapons and ammo; we will be fine."

I don't reply because there's no point, and I've realised she's totally crazy and totally doing this whether I go with her or not.

We come to the edge of a car park that is lined with trees, and we all move quickly behind them, using them as a shield to get as close to the front doors as we can.

Once we come to a stop, we do a quick scan of the area, but there is no movement.

"She's in there," Zoey states as she fixes her eyes on a window upstairs and points. I look up and see a woman with short blonde hair, glasses pushed up on her head, and a phone by her ear as she stands there, her mouth moving as she speaks.

She looks older than I expected her to, maybe in her forties. She turns away from the window, her back to us as she continues to hold the phone.

"We're gonna KO this bitch," Zoey says as she pulls her gun from her pocket, and I notice it already has a silencer on it.

"And how are we going to get in there without being seen?" I ask, because the minute we walk out of these trees, we are going to be spotted.

"We're not," she says before she charges out and into the open, racing for the front doors.

"Oh my fucking God," I whisper to myself before I dart out after her, praying that we don't get shot down before we've even started.

Zoey gets to the side of the house and flattens herself against the wall. I join her seconds later and do the same thing on the other side, adrenaline rushing through me.

I look back to the trees and see the guys are still standing there. They didn't follow us, but then Zoey is doing some kind of signal shit with her arms and the men start to scatter until I can only see one of them left standing there.

And then I'm almost shocked to death as the front door opens, the side closest to me swinging back and hitting me. I suck in a breath and stifle my grunt as pain slams into me. I turned my head, but the door hit the side of my head and my cheek, my chest, my legs—my whole fucking body so it seems.

I wait as I expect a head to pop around and say 'coo-ey' before dragging me to my death, but it doesn't. Instead, a tall man walks to the driveway in front and then continues on down until I can no longer see him. I allow myself a breath of relief, but that is short-lived as Zoey peers around and grabs my hand, dragging me behind her and inside.

She moves us along a hallway, and when I hear footsteps echoing behind us, she darts into a door on the left, moving us to a dresser and indicating for me to crouch behind it. I don't need telling twice as Zoey disappears behind one of the long curtains that frames a big bay window.

The footsteps get closer, and I hold my breath, moving my hand to the gun tucked into my sock so that I can pull it out and use it quickly if needs be.

Clip. Clop. Clip. Clop. Closer they get, and just when I think that they are about to come in this room and spring us from our hiding places, they walk on by until there is total silence.

I close my eyes and let my head fall back against the wall.

Zoey moves from behind the curtain and comes over to me. "You okay?" she whispers.

"Oh yeah, just peachy," I reply sarcastically. "What is the plan here?"

"Shoot the bitch."

"And that's it?"

"Pretty much," she says as she stands tall and moves to the doorway. I join her and then she's gesturing for us to move out. I only really have her guidance to go by at this point, so I follow and stay alert. I watch behind us, my head constantly turning as Zoey takes us back to the stairs.

She points and I pray that we get up there undetected.

We move as quickly and as quietly as we can. We're so fucking open right now, and I don't like it. It's just asking for trouble.

We're halfway up when I hear a voice come from the top.

"Well, well, well…" Oh Christ, we've been caught. This is it. Shit. "What have you got to say for yourself?"

I gulp and look up, because if I am about to die then I at least want to lock eyes with my maker. But to my surprise, there's no one there. Zoey looks back at me and shrugs before we move again, managing to get to the top.

Another long hallway. Brilliant. No hiding places except for the rooms on either side, and she could be in any one of them.

"So you gave me up and told them where to come?" the voice says, and my heart literally tries to pound its way out of my chest.

Footsteps start to come from behind, but there is no way we can turn around now, we're in too deep.

"Shit," I say as Zoey starts to jog, the quietness of our footsteps forgotten as we hurry to try and get to the other end and away from whoever is behind us. They're running too now, and my heart is racing, my lungs burning for air as we tear our way along. And just when we're about to reach the end, two men appear from a room to the right, and within seconds, I'm clamped against one of them, their hands immobilising me as they wrap their arms around. I struggle, I squirm, and I kick my feet, but this guy is strong, and I know that I am not getting free.

"Let go of me, you asshole," Zoey says from behind, but I know that is no use. There's no point in fighting. No point in yelling. We came here and now we just have to ride this out, and hopefully, we get to live at the end of it.

I'm taken back to the halfway point of the hallway, and then through a door on my left. And there, standing by the window still, is Jessica.

She has no expression on her face as she stares at me, the hatred clear in her eyes.

I'm taken to the side of the room where there are chains attached to the wall.

"No," I whisper as I try to do anything to get free, but when I feel the chains clamp around my wrists, I know it's too late. They don't bother with my feet, but then why would they? I'm not getting out of these cuffs anytime soon.

"Zoey," Jessica says, as if this is a friendly meet. "What a surprise." Her voice is high-pitched, and I don't know whether she's putting it on whether that's actually how she sounds.

"Quite," Zoey replies, no cheer to her voice whatsoever.

"So, to what do I owe the pleasure of this visit?" Jessica asks as she stays where she is, her arms folded over her chest.

"Oh, you know, just thought it would be good to catch up," Zoey says, and I clench my teeth as Jessica laughs. It's a sound akin to fingernails on a chalkboard. Jesus, how the hell did Nate ever work with this woman? Her voice and laugh alone would have driven me nuts.

"Don't tell me you miss me?"

"Cut the bullshit, Jessica. We both know I came here to end you." Zoey cuts straight to it, no beating around the bush.

"And you brought along a treat," Jessica says as she walks forward and then stops just out of kicking reach. The two guys that grabbed us guard the door, and I bet there are more shady bastards lurking around the place. This woman doesn't strike me as someone who would be left with just a couple of minions. She knows what Nate is like, she knows his world, and she knows to protect herself.

Although, I don't know if there would be enough protection in the world to stop Nate if she hurts either of us.

"So, you're the one he chose," she ponders as she looks me up and down. "Cute, but that's probably where it ends."

Zoey scoffs and I pray that she keeps her mouth shut so I can try and get a read on this bitch.

"Tell me, does it feel good to fuck what belongs to me?" she asks, cocking her head to the side slightly.

I don't answer her. She wants a reaction, and I will be damned if I give her one.

"Hmm. Shy, are we? Of course you're not, otherwise you wouldn't have come here, so stop playing stupid games and answer me," she says, but again, I say nothing.

Come on, Nate, please get here. Please.

"He's a fine specimen of a man, huh?" she continues as I bite my tongue. "Rock hard abs, thick thighs, and the best ass I've ever seen."

Okay, so bunny boiler it is. She's got it bad, and she's clearly unhinged, so I'm guessing that whatever pain she is planning to inflict on me is going to be bad.

"I don't like when others play with my toys," she says, and I struggle to remain as quiet as I have been.

"Jesus, Jessica, can you cut it with the details... that is my brother you're talking about," Zoey says, and Jessica has clearly had enough of her mouth as she clicks her fingers and one of the burly men comes over, whipping a roll of tape out of thin air it seems, and ripping some off before he covers Zoey's lips. She kicks out at him to try and stop him, but he just sidesteps and then he's taking his place back by the door. Zoey's cries of rage are now muffled, and Jessica chuckles quietly.

"Always had a motor mouth that one," she says, and I swear I would inflict so much pain on her if I could only get out of these damn chains.

"I bet you thought you hit the jackpot when you married him, huh? Bet you thought all of your Christmas' had come at once.

Well, I'm here to make sure you never put your hands on what is mine again."

Another click of her fingers has the other guy walking over and standing beside her.

"I think Mrs Knowles needs a taste of what it's like when you take something that isn't yours," Jessica says, and my blood runs cold at the manic look in her eyes. "Have your fun first before you finish her off."

I struggle to breath.

I struggle to think.

I struggle to do anything other than watch in horror as the second guy comes over and quickly picks up my legs, bounding them together with his arms as the other fucker wraps rope around them.

"Don't worry, princess, you'll pass out before they really get going, and then you'll be completely at their mercy," Jessica says with a loud laugh, and I have to stop myself from throwing up, swallowing the bile back down because being taken out of here with sick all over myself would be an even sadder state of affairs.

Zoey looks at me in horror, her legs and arms moving wildly, but it's no use. She won't be able to get free.

"And if you're thinking about those biker men coming to rescue you, then don't. They're all dead," Jessica tells us, and I swear I see pain in Zoey's eyes. "Ruin her," Jessica tells the guys before my arms are uncuffed and quickly twisted behind my back. I'm lifted by the one of them, but before we get any further, a dark figure appears in the doorway, blocking the exit. The guy has black hair, a scar running down the side of his face from his eyebrow to his top lip. He's tall and of a fairly decent build, and those eyes... no light in them at all, and that is where pure evil lurks. A dark brown colour that hinges on being black, and only the light from the windows shows the difference. The sly smile on his face chills my blood even more.

Who the fuck is this guy?

"Hi, sis," he says as he looks at Zoey, and my eyes widen with surprise.

Sis?

What the hell?

"It's been a long time," he says, crossing his arms over his chest as he leans against the door frame.

I can hear Zoey's muffled cry of shock behind me.

"Take the tape off of her mouth," he says, and the guy not holding me goes to Zoey, and I hear the tape ripped off of her skin and I wince.

"Wha... How... Wh..." Zoey tried to piece together a sentence as I hear her breathing deepen.

"You didn't really think I'd just disappeared never to be seen again, did you?" he asks her, his voice gruff with no kindness there whatsoever.

Zoey remains silent, and I can only imagine it's from shock— pretty much what I'm feeling right now because I had no idea that they had another brother. But there has to be a reason for that, and all I can think is that he was cut out of their lives.

"I can see your brain working overtime," he says to me. "So, I'll fill you in quickly. I'm Lucas Knowles, and everything Nate has should be mine. The money, the power, the glory... he doesn't deserve it. But I was made into the black sheep of the family when I killed our parents because I was sick of waiting for them to die."

I gasp at his crudeness and at the sheer lack of emotion in his voice.

He killed their parents?

Christ. This man has absolutely no morals if he's willing to do that off his own back.

"Nate was always the fucking favourite. Always the one that was lined up to be the most powerful of them all. And when I slit their throats, I thought I had it in the bag, but then shit went wrong and I had to flee.

"Turns out, no one really liked me much, and they all chose Nate over me. So, I bided my time, went underground, kept silent, and now, here I am, ready and waiting for him to come here to rescue you both... and he won't even see the trap as he comes in here. He won't be thinking clearly, and it will pave the way for me to capture him and torture him before he meets his maker."

"No," I cry out, the first words I've spoken in a while because the thought of him not being here kills me. I might as well be dead if he is.

"Aww, isn't that sweet... You want me to keep him alive for you?" he says in a weird-ass voice that sends an uncomfortable shudder down my spine. "Too fucking bad, princess. His death has been on my mind for years, so as soon as I feel as if I have tortured him enough, I'm going to take my shot."

"No, please, you can't——"

"Oh, I think I can," he says, cutting me off. "You see, I've been watching him for years, just waiting for my moment, and then you came along, and just like that, I knew how to hurt him so bad that he would never recover," he says, and I grit my teeth to stop from screaming out.

"Just think how he will cope without his wife and his sister. Doesn't bear thinking about really, does it?" he taunts, and I look at the guy that is supposed to love the both of them because they are his blood. He did not get Nate's looks, he did not get Zoey's compassion, he didn't get either of their thirsts for life... all he got was a thirst for evil. I've known him all of a few minutes and I can see it as plain as day.

"It'll make him careless to know that I have you both," he says with a grin.

"Lucas, please don't do this," Zoey pleads, and I can hear the hurt and pain in her voice.

"Why not? Because we can all be one big happy family?" He laughs cruelly at her. "I don't fucking think so. Now, take her away and make sure we hear her screams," he says to the two guys, and then he's stepping aside and we're leaving the room, my heart pounding with terror, my body trembling with shock, anger and fear.

And then it comes to me.

The guy from Purity and his words from that night... *"Hopefully the boss will let me, once I have delivered you to him because I would love nothing more than to fuck Nate Knowles' woman."* Oh my God, his boss... he... Lucas. Jesus Christ, I can't believe I haven't thought of that until now. I could have passed that onto Nate, it was clearly fucking important... and now it's too late. I can't tell him anything because there is a very real possibility that I will never see him again.

How the fuck am I going to get out of this one?

How is anyone meant to warn Nate of what awaits him?

"Oh, and don't worry, Kat... I'll take good care of Nate once you're gone... when he's all alone and needs some attention... you know, before Lucas puts a bullet in his brain," Jessica shouts from behind me, and I blink back the tears that sting the backs of my eyes. It's no good crying, that won't get me anywhere. Why would she go to all of this trouble to get Nate's attention, just so Lucas could kill him?

It makes no sense, and clearly, she's more fucked-up than I was led to believe.

I make sure to take in where we are going, because if there is any chance of me getting out of here, then I need to know where to go. I'm taken back down the stairs and then we're moving through a door to the left and down more stairs, these ones concrete and a slow drip of water seeming to echo all around.

If these men touch me, then I would rather die anyway. I wouldn't want to live after being tainted by them. I couldn't bear to be with the memory of any other hands on me except for Nate's.

Christ, I spent so much time hating him and not enough time loving him.

I wasted valuable minutes of our lives, and now it all feels like it was for nothing.

A lone lightbulb comes to life as we reach the bottom, and I see nothing except for a bed in the middle of—what appears to be—the basement.

There are handcuffs at the top and the bottom, the sheets are filthy, and the pillows have seen better days.

Fucking hell, how many women have they had down here?

I'm taken to the bed, and I fight with everything I have to try and get these guys off of me, but I end up led down, both hands and feet cuffed and spread apart.

They both look down on me, and the one to my right speaks first. "I get the first go."

"No way, man, you had the first hit on the last one," the other guy argues.

"Yeah, and good job too, because she was ruined once you'd had her," the first guy says, and my eyes look around for anything that could distract them. But of course, there is nothing as it is bare. Nothing to help, nothing to take their attention off of me. Just a lonely old bed and a woman that got in way too deep cuffed to it.

"I hope you don't mind a bit of pain, because I like to fuck with knives," the second guy says and my heart plummets into my stomach. "Better than lube. Free-flowing and no need to keep reapplying."

Oh my God.

No.

Please no.

This can't be how I go out.

Nate, please come and rescue me. Please find me. Please get these men away from me.

But as more minutes tick by and the first guy whips out his dick, I feel the hope die inside of me. Guy number two rips my top in half and cuts through the middle of my bra, leaving my breasts exposed to them.

"Oof, would you look at that, Alf? Perky tits and enough to fill your hands," guy number two says—so now I have one of the fucker's names to add to my last memories. Wonderful.

"Please don't do this," I manage to say, realising that I actually can fucking speak, and my mouth hasn't been taped or gagged. The shock must have rendered me speechless, but I need to try and appeal to these guys somehow. "If you let me go, I'll make sure Nate leaves you both alone. He won't come after you, I promise."

They both stare down at me for a second before bursting into laughter.

"Oh, man, you may be pretty, but you have no fucking brains,"

Alf says, dick still in hand. "There is no way that Nate would let us go. We know who he is, and we're going to enjoy fucking his tight wife before we disappear from here for good. We're not sticking around for him to find us, but you… well, you were just too good an opportunity to pass up."

Alf licks his lips and starts moving his hand up and down as guy number two—whose name I still don't know—starts to unbutton my jeans. I twist and turn from side to side as much as I can, but when he pulls a knife from under the bed and holds it to my pussy, I stop.

My body freezes as he runs the knife down the zip.

"That's better," he says with a smirk as Alf grunts on the other side of me.

I swallow down more bile and fix my eyes on the ceiling. I need to zone out, make myself numb while they defile my body. I don't want to think. I don't want to feel.

I cast my mind back to the first time I met Nate. How I thought he was hot, how I thought he was sexy despite being a bad man—or so I was led to believe. Because he's not all bad. And yeah, he may only show his softer side to me, but that was all I needed to fall hard and fast, even if I did deny my attraction to him for months.

Tears stream down my cheeks and I cry silently as I feel my jeans being tugged.

I think about the time that Nate first made love to me. How he caressed me, touching me so gently as if I would break. How his mouth made me forget everything else.

My heart aches as I think about not being with him again. Not holding him. Not having him pull me close. Not feeling his lips on mine.

The tears come faster; my cheeks drenched with my turmoil.

I should have told him that I loved him sooner.

He's the only person in the world that has ever shown me true love, and for that, I will always have the memory of being the centre of someone's world.

"I can't get these off of her," guy number two says as I tune back in, feeling the tugging on my jeans stop.

"Uncuff her then. I'm ready to stick my dick in her," Alf says, but I don't look at him and his manky dick. I can't. It's just too gross for words.

"Fuck's sake," the other guy grumbles, and then I feel him place his hand on my ankle. He's unlocking the cuffs? Oh my God, he's unlocking the cuffs! It may only be the ones securing my legs in place, but my brain goes back into survival mode as I realise what I can do to buy myself some more time—even if it will only be minutes. Thank fuck for tight skinny jeans.

I wait, I bide my time, and when the fucker thinks I'm not going to react, I swing my right foot around and kick him straight in the dick, as hard as I can.

He shouts out loud and drops to his knees, his cheeks puffed out, his face red and his eyes watering.

"You fucking—" He doesn't get to finish his sentence because he slumps to the floor and passes out.

Oh my God.

"You bitch," Alf says, and I don't have time to process what is happening as he jumps on top of me, his dick on display and threatening to touch my skin as he leans over and slaps me across the face. Once, twice, three times. The force of each hit has my head feeling dizzy, the pain blasting through my face, but I clench my teeth and take another hit. I won't beg this asshole to let me go because I know he won't.

"I'm going to fucking ruin you," he snarls. He grabs his dick again and starts to shuffle up me. "I'm going to come all over your pretty face and then I'm going to stick it in you before he wakes up and disfigures you… pussy and face."

And as he starts to pump himself again, I scream out loud. It's all I have left to do. I can't move because he's too heavy. I can't escape because I'm still cuffed. All I have is my voice, even if it won't help me.

"GET OFF OF ME," I shout again and again and again.

"Shouting won't help you, but I kinda like it. Makes me feel like I've worked for my reward," Alf says, a sadistic grin on his face. Jesus, he gets off on this?

His body shudders and he closes his eyes. And just when I hear his breathing change, everything goes silent, and he collapses forwards on me before rolling off to the side and landing on the floor.

My brain frantically tries to work out what just happened, but when I look around the room and see Nate stood on the bottom step, I let out a cry of relief.

He made it.

He came for me.

He saved me.

"Nate," I whisper as he makes his way over, taking in my half naked state, my jeans which are unzipped and my—probably—red cheeks from the slaps.

"Fucking hell," he breathes as he goes to the cuffs keeping my hands in place. "Key?"

"The other guy had it," I say as I nod to the floor. "He's not dead."

"He fucking will be," Nate grates out as he rounds the bed and looks for the key. He finds it somewhere near the guy, but I can't quite see as the tears blur my eyes.

Nate leans over me and I feel the cuffs being undone, freeing my wrists from their restraints, and I waste no time in throwing myself at him, wrapping my arms around his neck and sobbing into his shoulder.

"I'm sorry," I whisper through my sobs. "I'm so sorry."

"Shhh, it's okay. I've got you," he says soothingly as he holds the back of my head to him, moving me off the bed and wrapping my legs around his waist.

I cling onto him because he is my fucking lifeline. I don't want to let go, but when I hear a grunt from behind, I know that I will have to, so Nate can end the other asshole's life.

"I need to—"

"I know," I say, cutting Nate off, knowing he needs to do this. I let my legs fall and I shakily stand, but he only lets go of me when he knows I'm going to be able to support myself. He takes off his jacket and wraps it around me, because my top and bra are shredded on the floor.

He places a light kiss on my forehead and squeezes my shoulders gently before walking around me and to the cretin on the floor.

He's pulled himself up on the side of the bed, not yet realising that Nate is here.

He grunts before shifting to a standing position, squinting as he does, his eyes going from the bed to me stood on the other side.

"How the fuck did you get over there?"

"That would be my doing," Nate says from behind him, and immediately his eyes go wide and the bit of colour that was left in his cheeks drains completely.

"Oh shit."

"Yeah, oh shit indeed," Nate says as he swiftly picks up the knife on the floor and proceeds to shove it up the guy's ass. His face contorts with pain as he falls forward onto the bed.

I hear footsteps on the stairs and turn to see some of Nate's guys coming down.

"Make him suffer," Nate tells them before he comes back over to me and lifts me back up. I wrap myself around him once again as we leave the basement to the sounds of howls of pain. I can't even feel sorry for him because he deserves everything he gets. If that makes me a mean person, then so be it, but he was going to use that knife on me and rape me, so I think his punishment is deserved.

"Didn't you want to be the one to kill him?" I ask Nate as I rest my hands on his shoulders and hold his eyes.

"Usually, yes, but getting you out of here is more important," he tells me, and there goes my heart. It's all his, and it always will be.

He carries me out and to his car which waits just outside the doors. I see Zoey is already inside, and I breathe a sigh of relief.

"And Jessica?" I ask.

"She's dead," Nate tells me.

"Your brother?"

"Dead."

"And was there any sign of Stefan?"

His jaw clenches, and his silence tells me all I need to know. Stefan is dead too.

"I'm so sorry," I say as his pain becomes mine and I place a light kiss at the corner of his mouth. "Let's go home."

Nate

As we make our way back home, I try to expel the anger that still runs rampant through my body.

Lucas.

Jessica.

Zoey.

Kat.

Stefan.

Lucas had been working with Jessica. She turned on me when she knew she couldn't make me fall for her or let her suck my dick. Woman scorned and all that… except she wasn't scorned because she was never mine, and I sure as shit was never hers.

When I turned up at The Lodge, making my way as quietly as I could through the place, I knew that I needed to stay focussed to get the two women that mean more than anything to me out alive. Being a hard-faced bastard all of these years came in quite handy, because I was able to turn my emotions down a notch and tap into my deadly side. The side of me that I have perfected over the years. The killer inside of me knew what he had to do in order to save Kat and Zoey and make sure I lived too…

I COULD HEAR a female voice as I made my way along the hallway. I had quietly taken out anyone standing guard on my way here, and my men were taking care of the rest that were lurking about the place. The beauty of a silencer is that your enemies don't even get an inkling of you creeping up behind them to end their life. And Jessica sure as hell will have no idea that she has been left open and unprotected as I come for her.

I pause outside the room as it all goes quiet, and then another voice has rage searing through me like a wildfire.

"Baby sis, I'm sorry it had to end like this… well, actually, I'm not really, and I will take great pleasure in finally bringing Nate to his fucking knees. It's his turn to beg for mercy, beg for life, but I'll never give him that.

"I'll torture him until he struggles to breath, and then I'll rip out his fucking heart and lodge a bullet in his brain at the same time, because I couldn't decide which ending was better, so I'll just go with both."

Motherfucking Lucas.

"Lucas, you promised me that I could have my fun before you ended him," I hear Jessica say.

"And you can. You can jump around on his dick as much as you like until I decide that it is enough," Lucas says, and I can hear the warning in his tone.

"You two are fucking sick," I hear Zoey say, and my heart thumps a bit harder hearing that she can speak, and I pray like fuck that she is okay.

"You always knew this about me, sis, and I never pretended to be anything else," Lucas replies, no shame, no fucks given. *"And you know what else, dear sister of mine?"*

There is a pause and I hear feet shuffling.

"I'm going to make sure that I retell the story to him over and over again about how his pretty little wife was raped repeatedly as she begged for her life."

That's it. That's where my patience fucking ends.

I stand up and move to the doorway, my gun trained in my hands and ready to fucking shoot.

Lucas has his back to me, as does Jessica, neither of them paying the least bit of attention to anything other than Zoey because they think they have this in bag, and it's made them sloppy.

I would love to torture Lucas, but there is no time. I see that Kat isn't in here and his words have me desperate to find where she is. So, I aim the gun and pull the trigger, the bullet landing in the back of his head and his body dropping to the floor. Pretty boring ending really, but I had to act fast.

I turn the gun on Jessica as she whirls around, her mouth dropping open and her eyes wide with shock.

"Nate," she whispers as her hands come up in front of her. *"Please… I didn't… Please don't…"*

"Spare me the fucking pity party," I spit as I walk into the room, my eyes quickly sweeping behind the door to make sure that no nasty surprises are lurking.

"You fucked with the wrong brother," I say, and I am about to pull the trigger, when Zoey shouts, "No, Nate."

I pause my finger and move my eyes to my sister, who has been chained up like a fucking animal.

"Let me do it," she whispers, and I can see the worry in her eyes. Worry for me. Worry at the thought of me killing a woman.

I'm not a pussy. I would kill Jessica and then eat my fucking dinner later like it was nothing… but on the inside, I don't know how I would feel. Killing a woman is on another level. It's something I have never had to do. And in order to save me, my baby sister is offering me an out.

"Get the key, let me out of these cuffs, and then I'll kill her," Zoey says, and I can see how determined she is to do this. "It won't be my first time," she adds on, shocking the shit out of me. My eyes widen slightly, and Zoey nods her head. She's killed someone? What the fuck? When? Who? How? But now is not the time for questions, I can ask those later.

"Where's the key?" I bark at Jessica, and she quickly scrambles to a desk in the corner, opening a draw and retrieving the key that will release my sister. "Unlock the cuffs," I order, all the while keeping my gun on her. She quickly does as I ask, and then Zoey is free, the chains with the cuffs clanking to the floor.

"Oh, I'm going to enjoy this," Zoey says as she punches Jessica in the face. Jessica drops like a sack of shit to the floor, and Zoey walks over to me, taking the gun from my hand and training it on Jessica. "Bye bye, Jessica. Sweet dreams." And then Zoey pulls the trigger, and Jessica's whimpering stops.

Silence fills the room, but I don't have time to waste as I turn to Zoey and ask, "Where's Kat?"

THE SIGHT of Kat on that bed will forever fucking haunt me.

Her clothes ripped from her body. Her limbs cuffed to the bed. And that asshole on top of her with his dick out.

I shake my head, needing to calm myself, because it's over. They're all dead. They're not going to hurt her now. But it doesn't stop the images flashing through my mind.

I can feel the tension rolling off of me in waves, and when Kat places her hand on my thigh, squeezing gently, I feel some of it ebb away.

She's here.

She's mine.

She loves me.

She's the only woman in the world who can calm me.

And I'm going to make this up to her... I just hope that what happened here doesn't drive a wedge between us and the life that we are just starting to make together.

Chapter Thirty

Kat

I GET into the bathtub and sit down, hoping it will relax my aching body and stop the recurring thoughts of what would have happened had Nate not shown up when he did.

I try to clear my mind, needing the peace that won't seem to come.

I need to forget. Need to erase it all from my memories.

I know it's only been an hour since we left The Lodge, and of course it is going to be raw, but I'd rather eradicate the pain right fucking now.

My eyes are sore from crying, my cheeks aching from being hit.

I don't know if being alone right now is what I need, but I'm saved from myself as the door opens and Nate walks in, coming to the side of the tub and crouching down.

He looks almost broken, and it sends a pang to my heart.

I feel like I have betrayed him and hurt the trust between us.

His eyes focus on the bubbles, and he leans his arms on the side of the tub, resting his chin in the middle.

"I'm sorry I never told you about Lucas. I just... I guess I never expected him to sneak his way back here and take a pop at me, so I never thought it was relevant... and I hate talking about the bastard."

"It's okay," I say softly, because I don't need to hear an explanation. Lucas killed their parents and then came back to kill Nate. I don't need to listen to how or why. I just know that he is better off dead with no possibility of coming back. I see Nate's shoulders sag slightly with relief. Maybe he thought I would be pissed off that I didn't know? But really, after everything we have been through, it's not important—especially now that he's gone for good.

"Zoey told me that she made you go with her. She told me she took your phone and then threatened to go on without you when you wanted to wait for me," he says, sadness filling his eyes.

"And all I can really say is I'm so fucking sorry, Kat," he says as he chokes on a sob. "I never should have brought you into this world. I never should have put you in harm's way..."

I'm sitting up straight and moving towards him so fucking fast, placing my hands on his shoulders, the water soaking right through his shirt.

"Don't say that," I tell him, feeling like my heart is being ripped in two from his words alone. "I belong here, with you." I see a tear fall down his cheek and it pains me to see him like this. Hurting. Suffering. Blaming himself.

I wipe the tear away with my thumb and look at my beautifully broken man. My husband. My enemy once upon a time, but now my whole fucking world.

"Don't you dare blame yourself for any of this. And Zoey just thought she was doing right, she wanted to protect you because she knew you wouldn't be able to cope with killing a woman."

"But if I hadn't made you marry me——"

"Then I would still be living a shitty existence not knowing what this love ever felt like," I say, interrupting him. "You saved me," I whisper as my eyes fill up again, even though I didn't think it was possible to cry anymore. But this time, it's in a different way. It's not because I'm scared and in pain. It's because my love for him is so fierce, so true, that I could never be without it.

"You saved me too," he whispers against my lips, and fuck... if I wasn't a goner before, I would be now.

"Come in with me," I say, and he kisses my lips before standing up and discarding his clothes. He steps into the tub, and we take up our usual position of him sitting behind me, his arms wrapped around me, holding me to him.

We lay like that for I don't know how long. Just being with each other. And I appreciate every single second of it.

Nate

I don't know what I did to deserve the love of Kat.

I mean, I made her marry me. I forced her to live this life. And she loves me despite all of that.

Something changed between us all those weeks ago. She let me in. She chose to forgive me for what I had done. And in doing so, she changed me.

The only person I ever cared about before her was my sister. She was my family and the one person I would have protected to the ends of the earth.

But Kat made me realise that I wanted to do that for her as well. And when I love, I love fiercely, and thank fuck she seems to like that.

I'm not going to lie and pretend that I'm not pissed at my sister for putting both of them in the firing line, but I also understand why she did it. And I know I shouldn't have let her kill Jessica, but I knew something had changed in her a few weeks ago. I saw it in her eyes that day in my kitchen. I knew she had done something that she couldn't ever take back, and it turns out that she had beheaded some guy that had been pawing at her as she made her way back home from a dinner date in town. Turns out, it was the guy she went for dinner with, and he turned out to be a predator.

So, she took matters into her own hands and cleaned the mess up herself. I'm a little shocked she never told me, and that she dealt with it herself, I mean, that's what I'm here for, to clean up her messes and deal with anyone who causes her harm. But with everything that has been going on, I guess she felt she couldn't come to me, or that she didn't want to bother me.

I need to make more of an effort because I have dropped the fucking ball recently.

Zoey is staying in one of the guest bedrooms, and Kat is still sound asleep in our bed. I'm sat in my office, processing everything that went down yesterday.

Jessica is dead.

Those two assholes are dead.

My brother is six feet under, and I really have no thoughts on that whatsoever. I cut the cord with him a long time ago. Popping a bullet in his head was all I was capable of because I needed to get to Kat more, but I wish I had been able to skin him alive and make him scream for mercy. Although, he probably wouldn't have ever screamed, he always liked pain, but I would have done my damndest to try and make him squeal. He always hated me. Was always jealous of me. And he made the mistake of thinking that I would be too preoccupied in my mind to be able to take him down. I guess the joke's on him because now he's as dead as a dodo and no one will mourn him.

And then there's Stefan. Dead. My right-hand man gone forever.

I sigh and drop my head in my hands as I realise that he isn't here anymore. My only friend—or as close as you can get to a friend in this world I live in. We had been friends a long time and his death has me questioning everything about this life I lead.

I nearly lost my sister. I nearly lost my wife. And I did lose my main guy.

Is this life for me anymore?

I'm not sure.

I need to grieve, but my hard-ass nature isn't letting me. I don't even know where to begin. I've lost guys before, and sure, it sucks, but I never cared for them. Never thought of them as family. They just worked for me, and they knew the score when they signed up and passed the vigorous tests I put in place to make sure they were up to the task.

But Stefan… he'd been with me since the beginning. Always there. Always had my back. And now he's gone.

I run my hands through my hair and fire up my laptop.

Kat and I never had a honeymoon, and I think the time has come for us to get away, take a break and just enjoy being together without any added worries of someone coming for my ass—or hers.

It doesn't take me long to book flights and a hotel to stay at, and of course, I booked a place for Zoey too. I'm not leaving her here to deal with this by herself. We need to stick together, like we should have done all along.

I call around a few of my guys, telling them that I will be gone for a few weeks from tomorrow, and I instruct them to let everyone else on the payroll know.

With Stefan gone, I delegate Ronan to be in charge, and he accepts the role eagerly.

Now all I have to do is tell the ladies in my life that they need to pack their shit and get ready to leave. But before I do, I need to say goodbye to Stefan.

Kat

I stand by Nate's side, holding his hand, squeezing gently as Stefan's coffin is lowered into the ground.

It's not even been twenty-four hours since his body was recovered, but Nate managed to quickly and efficiently organise an intimate send off to say goodbye to a man that stood by him through everything. I feel sad that he's gone, for Nate's sake, but I also feel sad that I never really got the chance to know him.

I look around at the guys circling the grave, and they all have their heads bowed, some even have their eyes closed.

Zoey didn't come today, because she's still struggling with what went down. Can't say I blame her in the slightest. It's been one hell of a rollercoaster over the last day.

"Ashes to ashes, dust to dust…" the vicar says as Stefan's coffin is lowered into the hole in the ground. What an awful way to go out. So young. So much life left to live. And I hate the thought that one day that could be Nate. With this life there are no guarantees, and he might be breathing today, but tomorrow, he could be taken from me.

The thought has me choking on a sob, and I feel Nate's hand let go of mine, and then his arm is around my shoulders as he pulls me to him. I hold onto the front of his jacket, feeling so fucking thankful that he is still here. I know I shouldn't be thinking like this at a funeral, but I can't help it. I still have my husband, and even with everything I know about how deadly this world is, I'll never leave his side.

I'll help him get through this.

I'll always be here for him.

Forever and ever.

Amen.

Chapter Thirty-One

Kat

I ZIP UP MY SUITCASE, having packed everything I need, and I am so ready to get out of here. We all need a break, and Nate couldn't have picked better timing. I'm pleased Zoey is coming with us—belated honeymoon or not—because she needs us right now.

I saw the look in her eyes when the bikers were shot dead. She was hurting, and there is way more to that story than them just owing her a favour. I won't push her though; she can tell me in her own time—hopefully.

I look at myself in the mirror and undo the shirt I'm wearing—which is Nate's because it brings me comfort. Pushing the fabric to either side of my body, I see the bruises that have started to form, marking me like a fucking dot-to-dot picture.

I sigh, my heart feeling heavy.

Nate hasn't said much today, just gave me a kiss and hug and told me of the plans to go away. He hasn't mentioned Stefan, and I have to admit that I am worried. It's not good to bottle shit up—I should know. Maybe he will open up when we're away? I hope so anyway.

I do my shirt back up and make my way to Zoey's room. She's been holed up in there all day and I need to see how she is.

I knock on the door softly and hear a faint, "Come in." I push the door open and see her led on the bed, her back to me as she lies on her side, facing the wall. She hasn't packed anything, and I know Nate came in here earlier to tell her we were going away.

"Zoey," I say as I move to the bed and sit on the edge, placing my hand on her shoulder. I feel her body judder with a sob.

"I'm okay," she chokes out.

"Except you're not," I reply, my heart hurting for whatever pain she's going through.

She rolls on her back, and I pull my hand away as I see her face is blotchy, her eyes puffy, her skin pale. There's no twinkle to her eye, no light.

"I just... I can't..." She trails off as tears fall down her cheeks and I grab her hand and squeeze it gently. Despite what happened, I don't hold her responsible. She was just doing what she thought was right at the time.

"Is it Lucas?" I ask, because it could be that, I guess, or it could be the other thing I'm yet to ask.

"No. I couldn't give a toss about him. He was evil, and the world is better off without him here."

Fair enough. I don't think anyone would argue that fact with her.

"The bikers... they were more than just a favour to you, weren't they?" I ask quietly, and even though I said I wasn't going to push her, I think she needs a little nudge.

She nods her head and starts to talk.

"Jason... he and I... we... had a thing. It had been going on for a few weeks. We were keeping it quiet until we knew where it was leading, but I know I was falling for him, and because of me and my stupid actions, he's dead."

"Oh, Zoey," I say as I reach for her and pull her up to a sitting position, embracing her in a hug.

"I don't want to be part of this world anymore, Kat, but I know there is no escape. Nate's been the crime lord for so long that I know he can't just make a clean break. There would be too many people wanting to take him down. But... we've lost so many people. Jason, Stefan, and more before that... I just... I don't think I can do this anymore."

I let her cry it out, just holding her, letting her tears dampen the shoulder of my shirt.

There's not much I can say. Nothing I can do to ease her pain except be there for her.

Because this is my family now.

Zoey and Nate.

I've never really had a family before. My mother was useless and my dad even more so. I never knew what being close to anyone felt like, until the Knowles blew into my life.

I always wanted a sister, and now I've got one.

I always wanted the love of a man who would put me above himself, and I have one.

And no matter what happens from here on out, I know that we will always look out for each other, because that's what a family does.

Nate

I didn't mean to listen in, but as I walked along the hallway and heard sobs coming from Zoey's room, I stopped and then Zoey started to speak.

"Because of me and my stupid actions, he's dead."

"We've lost so many people."

"I don't think I can do this anymore."

I had no idea that she had something going with one of the MC guys.

I had no idea that she wanted to leave all of this behind.

I had no fucking idea.

None.

But now that I do, I have a choice to make.

And if I'm going to do right by my family, then I have to make sure everything is tied up. Finished. Done.

Chapter Thirty-Two

Kat

THE BEACH IS GLORIOUS, the sun beating down on my face, and I love the quiet here.

Nate brought us to an island that is secluded but still has everything we need. The hotel is luxurious, and we have our own private section of the beach to do as we please.

We've been here for three days now, and even Zoey seems more relaxed. I know she's still hurting, but maybe, being so far away from home is helping her. Out of sight, out of mind, maybe?

I sip on the iced coffee that sits beside me on a little wooden table that is attached to the lounger I'm currently lying on. Zoey is led next to me, and Nate is in the sea, with a surfboard. Yes, my husband can surf, and he's bloody good at it. I watch him as he uses a paddle to move along, looking so at peace that it makes me smile.

He's relaxed more too since we've been here. It's doing us all good.

I could just picture us living out our days here, surrounded by the beauty of the tropical island. Picture perfect.

I continue to watch Nate as he moves, his balance unwavering, his abs on display for me to drool over.

"Put your tongue back in your mouth," Zoey says from beside me as she chuckles.

I avert my eyes to see her with a smirk on her face.

"I can't help it if my husband is the hottest guy I've ever seen," I tell her, knowing it will cringe her out.

"Can we not? I don't care to hear how my brother makes you all fucking girlie and shit," she says with a grimace, and I laugh loudly.

"You started it," I say as I sip my drink.

"Yes… well… now I'm ending it," she says matter-of-factly.

Comfortable silences stretches between us before Zoey speaks again. "You know, I could get used to this way of life."

"You mean the fine food, the peace, the quiet, and the fact that there is no drama?" I say.

"Exactly that."

I couldn't agree more, and I'm going to enjoy every single second before we have to go back.

I watch as Nate comes back to the shore, holding the surfboard under his arm and dropping it on the sand a few feet from us. Splashes of water hit me, and I squeal as the cold drops hit my skin.

"Fancy a dip?" Nate asks me, his head cocked to one side and mischief in his eyes.

"Sure," I say as I place my coffee down and stand up. "But you'll have to catch me first." With that, I take off running, hearing his laughter behind me. I run to the left and enter the trees, making my way through them, my heart pounding with excitement. I love the playful side of Nate, and it's come out more and more over the last few days.

I dodge trees, going deep into—what I can only describe as—a tropical forest. Colourful flowers surround me, the beauty of the island shining bright as I tear through. I breathe deeply as I hear his footsteps pounding behind me.

I didn't even have this much fun in my teens, for fuck's sake. But I'm making up for it now.

I wonder if Nate and Zoey used to do this when they were kids? Just have fun. Just be.

I hope so.

I chance a glance behind me, but the space is empty. I dart to the right and flatten myself against a tree trunk, desperately pulling air into my lungs.

I keep my ears pricked but I don't hear anything, and I can't see Zoey from where I am, the view shrouded by all the tree trunks and lush greens of the flower's leaves, along with the pinks, oranges and yellows of the petals.

I peer around the tree, but still see nothing before I am hauled against his hard body, his lips by my ear as he says, "Gotcha." I'm whirled around so I'm facing him, my back slamming against the tree trunk and his lips capturing mine.

Heat pools between my legs as he kisses me fiercely, like he needs me to breathe.

I pull him closer, needing more. Always needing more.

Moving my hand down, I push past his swimming shorts and fist my hand around his cock. He grunts into my mouth as I start to move my hand up and down, loving the feel of him growing hard for me.

I move my other hand into his hair, tugging hard, eliciting a deep, feral moan from him.

His fingers find my pussy, and moving my bottoms to one side, he pushes two fingers inside of me. I arch my back and lift my leg, wrapping it around him. He adds a third finger, stretching me as he moves his mouth down to my nipple, sucking hard through the fabric of my bikini top. I cry out, pumping my hand faster, gripping him tighter as his thumb connects with my clit, moving in circles, his fingers still inside of me.

I struggle to hold myself up as my legs start to tremble and Nate moves to my other nipple, lavishing the same attention on that one too.

I feel the pre-cum at the head of his cock, and I run my thumb over it, taking my hand out of his trunks and bringing my thumb to my lips, sucking his taste off of me.

"Fuck," he says as he lifts me up, my back scratching against the bark, but I don't care. He pushes his trunks down and pulls my bottoms to the side before he slams into me. "So. Fucking. Hot," he growls out as he pounds in and out, his power unrelenting.

I hold his stare, seeing everything he feels for me. Love, lust, want, need, protectiveness, it's all there.

My eyes want to flutter closed as he rubs my clit again, but I force myself to keep watching him, to be able to see the moment when I make him come undone.

His hand comes to the nape of my neck, and he threads his fingers through my hair, holding me as he brings my forehead to rest against his.

"All. Fucking. Mine," he whispers.

"Yes. All fucking yours," I tell him, and he groans, pounding even harder, pushing me even quicker towards my release. He pinches my clit, and I'm done. I clench around him, feeling him hit deep inside of me, dragging out my orgasm until I'm trembling so fucking hard. And then he's there, his lips smashing against mine as he releases inside of me.

A satisfied smile crosses my face.

I'm the happiest I have ever been, and I realise that no matter where we are, as long as I'm with him, I'm home.

Chapter Thirty-Three

Nate

"YOU READY TO GO LADIES?" I ask as I walk into the spacious living accommodation we have for the remainder of our stay. Zoey has her own suite on the opposite side of the hallway to us, but during the day, we're all spending time together wherever we are.

"Where are we going?" Zoey asks excitedly as she stands up and walks over to me.

"Just wait and see."

"Always such a stiff," she says, and I laugh. I never give anything away before I need to, and it has always driven her nuts. But this time, it's just to prolong the suspense—and hopefully the excitement that will follow.

Kat comes walking from the bedroom and looks fucking delicious in the dress she's wearing—which is white with a slit up each side that goes to mid-thigh, her tanned skin showing beneath, her hair down in natural waves and her face free of any makeup. Yeah, I'm going to eat that later.

"I'm ready," she says with a smile, and I turn and lead the way before I turn into a fucking caveman and drag her ass to the bed—

or anywhere really. Doesn't have to be a bed, could be the goddamn street for all I care.

Shit. Calm down, Nate, no need for a boner right now.

We make our way out of the suite and down to the lobby, where I can already see the car I ordered waiting outside for us. This hotel is the best on the island, and all the staff are more than eager to help seeing as I tip pretty damn generously. No one here knows what I do, so no one looks at me with any fear, and I have to say, it's rather refreshing. Here, I can just be Nate. Not a crime lord. Not someone that has to inflict pain and suffering or kill anyone that crosses my path.

The car door is opened by the driver and the ladies get in the back, but I take the passenger seat so I can give directions to where we need to go.

I can feel the buzz coming from both of them as we start to drive away from the hotel, and it is bloody infectious because I feel buzzed too.

I've never relaxed this much in my life, and it's something I really didn't realise I needed until now.

We make our way through the town and to the outskirts of the island, taking a few turns here and there until we're moving up the driveway that will take us to our destination. No one asks any questions, and I smile as I see Kat and Zoey taking in our surroundings, their eyes wide with wonder.

I only hope that momentum keeps going for what I have planned.

As we move further up the driveway, a large house comes into view with balconies for the rooms on the second level, a fountain in the middle of the driveway, and the beach spread out in front of us.

"Oh wow," I hear Kat whisper behind me as we stop.

I get out of the car and open the back door for them before the driver can, and I tell him that I will call when we need a ride back to the hotel. Once we exit the car, he drives around the fountain and back down the way we came.

"This is so beautiful," Zoey says as she takes in the secluded beach, the waves rippling gently and the gardens that surround the path leading to the sand which have been tended to and are a lush green.

"Come on," I say as I take Kat's hand and pull her towards the house, Zoey following us.

I reach into my pocket and fist the key that has been burning a hole in my pocket for the last twenty-four hours. They have no idea what I have been up to, and I managed to do all of this whilst they were sleeping or catching a few rays of sunshine. It's amazing how much you can do and how quickly things can be accomplished when you have a shitload of money to flash in peoples faces.

We walk up the four steps to the property and I put the key in the lock, turning it and opening the door to—what can only be described as—paradise.

High ceilings, a sweeping staircase in the middle of the grand entrance hall, rooms off to the sides, a kitchen and dining space which takes up the back of the house, six bedrooms upstairs—all with an ensuite—and then there's the games room and office space which is built in the back garden and to the side. Not to mention the patio area with a built-in stone barbecue, a large stone table to match, and the infinity pool which looks onto the beach below. A little walk down gets you to the sand, the path having lights either side of it that come to life when it starts to get dark.

"Oh my God, Nate, what is this?" Kat says after her and Zoey have had a good look around the place, checked out all the rooms and made their way outside to join me on the patio.

I pour both of them a glass of champagne and hand it to them.

"You like it?" I ask as I sip a beer straight from the bottle. I don't do champagne, so a cold beer it is.

"Like it? It's fucking stunning," Zoey says as she walks over to the path to the beach and makes her way down it.

Kat is just looking at me with so many questions in her eyes. I wanted to tell them both together, but Zoey has made her way onto the sand, and I can tell her when she comes back.

"What is this?" Kat asks me, and I place my beer down on the glass table that is central to the seating area before I put my hands in my pockets and hope that I have done the right thing.

"Well… this is home, baby. Our home."

"Our what?" she whispers, and I suddenly feel a little nervous, like I jumped the gun here.

"Our home, if you want it to be."

She remains silent for a moment, just staring at me, and I can't get a read on her thoughts right now. Shit. I should have talked to her about it before coming here.

"But… but what about our life back in the UK?" she says quietly.

"What life?" I say with a shrug. "My life is wherever you are."

"You know what I mean, Nate. You have a business to run, you have obligations, you—"

"My obligations are you and my sister. Nothing else even comes close. And as for 'business,' I want out."

Her eyes widen and she gasps in shock. "You what?"

I take a step towards her, taking her glass from her and placing it beside my beer bottle before taking her hands in mine. "I want out. I don't want that life anymore. I'm done."

Her eyes fill with tears, and I don't know if they are the good kind or the bad kind.

"Really?" she says, like she can't believe what I'm saying.

"Really," I confirm with a nod of my head. "I want our life to be stress free. I want us to be able to do as we please, no threats following us around. We can't do that back in the UK, too many people know who I am. But here… here, no one knows me, no one knows my past, and we can just be free to live our lives as we see fit."

It's the truth.

I want the quiet life. Something I never entertained before Kat came along.

"And what if Zoey doesn't want this?" Kat asks, and dear God she is always thinking about someone else above her own needs.

"Well, she's free to make her own choice, I won't stop her, and I will make sure she is protected wherever she goes, but I think she's ready to leave it all behind," I say truthfully. It will kill me not having my sister close because I need to make up for the shitty times I've not been there for her like I should have been, but I would deal with it. I would live with whatever choice she made because it's time I started putting mine and Kat's happiness first.

"You really want this?" she asks, as if she needs more confirmation.

I move my hand up and cup her face, tilting her head a little more. "I really do."

A smile slowly spreads across her face, and I see all of the tension she must have been holding drain from her body.

"Then yes. Yes, let's do it."

My heart lurches at her words and I lock my lips to hers, kissing her slowly, our tongues merging together.

I lift her up and hold her to me, her legs wrapping around me in a move that I absolutely fucking love.

This is it.

This is us.

Our life.

Our happy ending.

She was my wrecking ball, and she smashed my ice-cold walls down, taking my heart and holding it tight in her grasp.

And I wouldn't have it any other way.

Chapter Thirty-Four

FIVE YEARS LATER

Nate

"DADDY," comes the sound of my daughter, Gracie, as she runs at me and launches herself into my waiting arms.

"Hey, sweetheart," I say as I hug her to me, never taking any of these moments for granted. She's already three—nearly four—and time is passing by too damn quick. Seems like five minutes ago she was a baby, and sometimes it feels like I've blinked and missed the last few years.

"Mummy is mad," Gracie whispers in my ear.

"Oh? Why?" I whisper back, because I appear to have turned into the soppiest sod alive since Gracie came into our world. I play games with her, spend as much time as I can with her, and becoming a dad was my greatest moment.

I'll never forget the way her tiny body felt in my arms when I first held her, and the first time she grabbed my finger in her hand, holding it tightly like she would never let go. Cold-hearted Nate is a thing of the past, and he has been replaced by a man that is totally under the fucking thumb. Dear God, who would have ever thought it?

"Because you left the wet towels on the floor again," Gracie says with a chuckle, her eyes twinkling. She really is a little version of her mother but with my sea-green coloured eyes.

"Oh sh—" I stop myself from finishing that word and replace it with, "Dear."

"She's really mad, Daddy."

"I'm not too worried, I can sweet talk your mum," I tell her, to which I hear a clearing of a throat behind me, and I wince. Gracie laughs at me, and I smile and give her a quick wink before turning around to look at the woman that takes my goddamn breath away every single day.

"Sweet talk me, huh?" Kat says as she tries to hide the smile that wants to break free.

"Why don't you go and get your swimming costume on, sweetheart, and then we can go in the pool," I say to Gracie before I lower her to the floor.

"Yay," she screeches as she runs into the house and disappears to go find her costume.

I fix my gaze back on Kat, and the fire that we had from day one is still there. It still burns bright, and fuck, I still can't get enough of her.

"So, how are you gonna sweet talk me, husband?" she says, her arms folded across her chest, her eyes raking up and down my body.

"Oh, I think you know how, wife," I tell her as I step towards her.

"Hmmm, I think I forgot," she says, and then I grab her, pushing her against the wall to the sounds of her laughing freely, happily.

"You need reminding of who you married?" I whisper in her ear before biting her ear lobe.

"Fuck yes," she says on a breath.

I smile against her skin as I plant kisses across her cheek, until my eyes are holding hers.

"Mouth," I remind her, but my issue with that died a long time ago. After everything that happened with Jessica, Stefan and my brother, I gave up trying to stop her potty mouth… but I didn't give up the threat because she fucking loved it—and still does.

"I'm on my way, Daddy," I hear Gracie shout, and I drop my head onto Kat's shoulder.

"I guess you'll just have to teach me that lesson later," Kat says with a chuckle before she slides along and saunters her fine ass over to the edge of the pool, taking her clothes off and revealing the one-piece she has on underneath that has circles cut out at the sides.

"Oh, it's on," I tell her before Gracie comes barrelling outside and jumps into the pool, splashing Kat as she does.

I laugh as Kat jumps in too and chases Gracie, who is squealing with so much excitement that it makes my heart ache in a good way.

I can wait to teach Kat that lesson, but it will be happening, and I will enjoy every single second of my wife beneath me, my cock inside of her, my mouth all over her, and her fingernails biting into my skin.

But for now, I'm happy and content to just be 'Dad.'

Nate Knowles.

Family man.

Husband.

And totally at peace.

THE END

Acknowledgments

I want to say a big big thank you to my readers and my supporters for picking up my books!

I love you all!

This is going to be short and sweet, because, book babes, I've got another book to write with a certain character that you've met in Wrecking Ball... (my lips are sealed... for now).

I hope you enjoyed Kat and Nate!

Until next time,
Much love,
Lindsey

About the Author

Lindsey lives in South West, England, with her partner and two children. She works within a family run business, and she began her writing career in 2013. She finds the time to write in-between working and raising a family.

Lindsey's love of reading inspired her to create her own book series. Her favourite book genre is romance, but her interests span over several genre's including mystery, suspense and crime.

To keep up to date with book news, you can find Lindsey on social media and you can also check out Lindsey's website where you can find all of her books:

https://lindseypowellauthor.wordpress.com

facebook.com/lindseypowellperfect

twitter.com/Lindsey_perfect

instagram.com/lindseypowellperfect

bookbub.com/authors/lindsey-powell

goodreads.com/lpow21

Printed in Great Britain
by Amazon

82504931R00129